RIDING WITH
A COWBOY

GLORIA DOTY

To love and be loved is a blessing.

Gloria Doty

This is a work of fiction. Names, characters, places, brands, media, and incidents are either the product of the author's imagination or are used fictitiously. Any resemblance to similarly named places or to persons living or deceased is unintentional.

ISBN-13: 978-1535581158

ISBN-10: 1535581158

ACKNOWLEDGMENTS

When I write about a subject or occurrence that I have not personally experienced, I rely on friends and 'friends of friends' to help me with the facts. I have never had anyone refuse to share their expertise. They are always willing and graciously answer my many questions. I am most appreciative of their assistance. Without them, the scenarios I write would not be believable and I am eternally grateful for their help.

Kidney Transplant: Jennifer Kleespie Trier
Medical: Kathy Sias-Head
Heart Trauma: Barbara Fischer
Rehab House: Kendra Wheeler
Chicago: Nancy Humphrey Haskins
Firearms: Todd Radke
Horses: Diane Butler Radke

Many thanks to my wonderful and talented team. Without them, these books would never be published.

Gwen Gades…cover design
Nina Newton…editor
Marilyn Reinking….proofreader
Adam Bodendieck…formatting

DEDICATION

Many friends and relatives have encouraged me on this writing journey, but the one person who has been my most ardent supporter is my youngest child, my daughter, Kalisha.

She pushes me to stay on task and make use of my time, often stating, "Mom, you should be writing."

She listens to my ideas and my complaints. She is enthusiastic about my accomplishments and never fails to tell everyone she meets, about the books.

She also reads them and writes a review for Amazon.

For her love, encouragement and support, I dedicate this book to her, Kalisha Renee Doty.

LIST OF MAIN CHARACTERS

*Calvin (Cal) Frasier   TX rancher
*Louisa (Lucy) Frasier   Cal's wife
*Samantha & Sean Getts   Cal's daughter and son-in-law
  Doug & Amy Getts   grandchildren

*Jackie & Gary Lincoln   Cal's daughter and son-in-law
  Gabriel (Gabe) Lincoln   grandchild

*Benson (Ben) & Candy Frasier   Cal's son and daughter-in-law
  Luke Frasier   grandchild

*Paul & Lynne Newsome   Lucy's son and daughter-in-law
  Jarrod & Annie Newsome   grandchildren

*Victoria (Vicki) & David Marsh Lucy's daughter and son-in-law
  Devon, Bethany & Olivia Rose   grandchildren

*Jerry Watkins   Cal's friend and attorney
*Phoebe Watkins   Jerry's wife and Lucy's best friend
*Leon Henderson   Lucy's brother
*Tess Frasier   Cal's sister

Prologue

LOUISA CROWDER WAS QUITE content with her life. She owned a successful business in Chicago, a beautiful home in Batavia, Illinois and her son and his family lived only a few blocks from her. All that changed when she went to visit her daughter, Vicki, and her husband in Texas. Lucy was a native Texan, having lived the first 20 years of her life on a ranch outside Magnolia, Texas.

Although she loved her home state, she also loved living in Illinois and working in the atmosphere of a big city like Chicago. While visiting, her world collided with the world of Calvin Frasier, a Texas rancher.

From that moment on, neither of their worlds were ever the same. Cal was a 62-year-old widower and Lucy was a 59-year-old divorcee. When their adult children weigh in on the budding romance with their objections and concerns and that becomes a problem, and the fact that Cal has a firm faith in Jesus Christ, while Lucy turned her back on God many years ago, it seems the obstacles are much too big to be overcome. Both Lucy and Cal have some secrets in their pasts that will eventually come to light and threaten any hope of their happiness and a future together.

Bring a Cowboy Home and *Loving a Cowboy* take the reader on a day-to-day adventure as the Frasiers face a myriad of problems in their lives, the lives of their children and their grandchildren. Suspense, drama, intrigue, love, understanding and real-life situations make these two books a compelling duo.

CHAPTER 1

CAL'S INNER ALARM CLOCK woke him as it had nearly every day of his life since he was in high school. He extricated himself from his curled up position around Lucy's body, trying not to disturb her. He sat on the edge of the bed for a bit before pulling on some pajama pants and going to the tiny kitchen in their shore-side cabin to make coffee.

When he came back to the bedroom, he drank his coffee while he watched Lucy sleep. Her bare shoulders above the edge of the sheet were tanned and smooth. Looking at her reminded him of their time together last night. Her dark hair was fanned out on the white pillow; her breathing was peaceful while a slight smile seemed to play around her lips. Perhaps she was dreaming of the last two weeks they shared on this island getaway. It was a trip he planned for their second anniversary and had actually been able to keep it a secret and surprise her.

The days had flown by, each one more exciting and fun than the one preceding it. Going back to their cattle and horse ranch in Texas might be anticlimactic after two weeks of perfect bliss.

Lucy stirred, rolled onto her back and opened her eyes. "What are you doing, Cal?" she asked sleepily when she saw him sitting in a chair, gazing at her.

"Looking at the most gorgeous woman in the world while she sleeps," was his reply.

Lucy started laughing and wiped her cheek. "I think the most gorgeous woman in the world drools when she sleeps," she said.

Cal smiled and held out a cup of coffee for her. "I don't mind."

Lucy sat up, pulling the sheet up a bit and reached for the cup. "You are way too good to me, Cowboy. You've had coffee ready for me every day since we got married, with the exception of when you were in the hospital after being shot, of course."

"Making coffee is such a small thing, Lucy. I would do anything in the world for you, and you know that, right?"

"Yes, I do know that. And your actions make me aware of that every day."

He moved to the bed and kissed her. "This is our last day in paradise," he told her. "What would you like to do today?"

"I think we've taken advantage of everything that's offered: scuba diving, horseback riding on the beach, deep-sea fishing, snorkeling, sailing, our version of tennis," Lucy chuckled, "and a trip through the casinos. I almost forgot, we went canoeing, too."

"It has been fun, hasn't it? Even though you refused to go parasailing," Cal told her.

"I didn't stop you from going, Sweetheart. I just said I wasn't doing that. Not in a million years."

"I think we ate our way through the two weeks, too. I haven't eaten that much or that variety of delicious food in a long time."

Lucy held the sheet back. "Why don't you get back under the sheets with me and we'll discuss what we're going to do today, okay?"

Cal put his coffee cup down and climbed back in bed. "So tell me, Lucy Mae," he asked as he waited for her to snuggle up to him and put her head on his shoulder, "what would be the best thing to do on our last day here?"

"I want to walk along the water's edge and say our morning prayers while we walk," Lucy began. "Then I want to buy a basket of the fresh fruit they have at the stand with the thatched roof and then...I don't know, I'm sure we'll think of some other activity while we walk."

She kissed him and headed to the shower, wrapping the bed sheet around herself and taking it with her as she went.

"What's up with the sheet wrapped around you, Lucy?" Cal laughed.

"I've always wanted to do that. You know, like women do in the movies; wrap themselves in the sheet as they walk away from the bed," Lucy told him. "I can't do that at home because then I'd have to put a new sheet on the bed. This was my chance. Here, someone else will replace the sheets."

*   *   *

"If you want, I'll spread some sunscreen on your shoulders and back, Cal," Lucy said, "but I don't want any today. My shoulders are still sore from yesterday. They hurt where the straps of my bathing suit were. I'll put a lightweight t-shirt on instead. That should protect me from the inevitable sunburn. I don't usually burn, but obviously, the sun is different here."

They walked barefoot along the water's edge. The sand was warm even this early in the morning and the small waves danced at their feet as they strolled, hand in hand. The turquoise water was as clear as glass for a long distance from shore. Where it became a little deeper, the color changed to an azure blue. The beach was nearly deserted and everything was quiet with the exception of the birds circling and the soft gurgle of the water as it lapped the sand.

Cal and Lucy said their morning prayers as they did every day, almost as a conversation with God. Cal had done this since he accepted Christ on a mission trip when he was in college. Lucy had to learn to 'talk' to God again, after turning her back on him for many years. In her wedding vows, she said God led her into Cal's arms and Cal led her back into the arms of her Savior. She meant it that day and still felt that way. Now, she couldn't imagine a day without God in it.

They began their conversation with God by giving thanks for every blessing in their lives: their grown children and grandchildren, their friends and the everyday blessings of health and prosperity, love and laughter, the wonders of new babies in their family and his protection in every area of their lives. Included in their prayers were specific requests for various people and situations. They asked for God's blessings on their ranch and their employees, their church family, the country and its leaders.

This shared prayer time was one more thing in their lives that bound them together and increased their feelings of being one person, in thought, actions and feelings.

"Are you certain you don't want to take this last opportunity to try parasailing, Lucy?" Cal laughingly asked when they finished their prayers.

She shaded her eyes and watched as some fearless soul sailed over them. "Nope. I will never regret not doing that. Thank you, anyway."

As she was looking up, she lost her footing in the sand and stumbled backward. Before Cal could catch her, she landed in the water. She grabbed Cal's arm and pulled him in with her. "Come with me. We may as well enjoy this gorgeous day and the water for a bit before we have to leave it all behind."

They walked out until the water was deep enough for swimming, then they swam for a while before walking back to the shoreline. Lucy had not planned on getting wet or swimming and only became self-conscious of how the wet shirt was clinging to her body when she saw the appreciative look on Cal's face as she walked out of the water.

"Come on, Sweetheart," she said as she grabbed his hand and hurried toward their cabin. "This is not a good thing."

Cal laughed at her, "Lucy, there's no one out here but the two of us and I think you would win a wet t-shirt contest any day of the week." As they walked, Cal asked her again what she would like to do on their last day of vacation.

"I want to do something you suggested a long time ago."

"I suggested it?" Cal asked, puzzled. "What was that?"

"Do you remember when it seemed like everything that could possibly go wrong...was going wrong?" Lucy asked him. "The rustling scheme was a huge concern, Jackie was upset about Gabe's autism diagnosis and Samantha's marriage seemed to be falling apart?"

"Yes," Cal said slowly. "But I don't remember what I said I wanted."

"This is a quote, my dear. You said, 'I want just one day not to think about any of those things. I want to get up in the morning, drink coffee with you, ride Cutter for a little while and then come home and make love to you all day long, with no phone calls or visits from anyone.'"

Cal nodded. "I do remember saying that. I was feeling overwhelmed by life and wanted... no, *needed...* a respite with you in my arms all day."

Lucy smiled at him and looked into his eyes. "We've already had our coffee, we've walked in the sand in place of riding Cutter and now we're back here. We can turn our phones off and spend the rest of our last day together, uninterrupted. How does that sound, Cowboy?"

Cal pulled her to him, removed the wet t-shirt and kissed her in a way that answered her question.

CHAPTER 2

CAL AND LUCY MADE SURE any gifts or souvenirs they purchased were sent home, which made packing an easy task. There was no more in their bags when they left than when they arrived two weeks ago.

As they were on the plane, waiting for take-off, Cal leaned his head back and told Lucy, "I think vacations are harder work than being at home. I'm exhausted."

Lucy leaned over and kissed his cheek. "Yes, some activities are exhausting, Honey."

Shaking his head, he winked at her and asked, "Seriously, did you have a good time?"

"Cal, I had a marvelous, never-to-be-forgotten time. Thank you so much for these two glorious weeks filled with sunshine, blue waters and new adventures. I can't even think of a way to say thank you."

"It isn't necessary to say thank you. I wanted to spend time alone with you. I love our kids and grandkids and everything about our life but I selfishly wanted you all to myself for a while."

Lucy took his hand in hers and traced his fingers, one by one. "Are you ready to be home?"

Cal smiled and nodded his head. "Yes, home sounds wonderful. On the one hand, I could stay in paradise with you forever, but on the other, it seems like it's been longer than two weeks since we've seen those grandbabies."

They used the seven hour flight home to discuss all the things they left behind when they opted for two weeks of solitude. When Cal whisked her away two weeks ago, he told her she had to agree not to think or talk about any issues at home while they enjoyed their idyllic getaway. For the most part, they did a good job of leaving it all behind, with only one phone call when they landed to let everyone know they arrived safely and another in the middle of the two weeks to check in. Cal called his son, Ben, before they left the island to let him know when to expect them home.

"You know, when I told Ben and Candy they should have a dozen children, I didn't know they were going to take me literally. When the twins are born in July, Luke won't be quite two years old yet. They'll have their hands full. I guess they'll reach a dozen faster if they have them two at a time," Lucy laughed.

Cal thought about his son, Ben, and his daughter-in-law, Candy. "They are good, loving, Christian parents. I am so proud of them. I wish the issues with Candy's parents could be cleared up. I feel like it's a weight on Candy's heart and she doesn't even know why."

"I know, but that has to come from Frank and Myrna. Just as you insisted that Leon tell me about the night he sold the Yellow Rose, Candy's parents have to be the ones to tell her about their mistakes. Maybe when they do, there can be repaired feelings between all of them."

Lucy was thoughtful for a minute, and then added, "When they decide to tell Candy, I think they should tell Ben first, because he's going to have to be there to comfort and love her and take away some of the pain that knowledge is going to cause. What do you think?"

"You're right. Ben will be shocked, too, but he will need to be Candy's support through the barrage of feelings she's going to have wash over her. It never fails to amaze me how actions that happen on the spur of the moment can have lasting effects years and even decades later; many of them devastating."

"I'm thinking of Leon and the son he fathered but didn't know about until a few years ago. He missed so much of Clint's life. We all make decisions we regret; some have more lasting effects than others."

Cal looked at her and said, "I only regret I didn't meet you sooner, because if I had, I could have loved you longer."

"I'm happy you didn't meet someone else in those ten years you were alone."

"I was waiting for you, Lucy and I didn't know it; at least, not until you told me to kiss you, on our first date. It was a slippery slope from there on."

Smiling at him, she said, "I truly believe we were meant to be together but not until all the other pieces of our lives were in place. You told me once if we had met earlier, we wouldn't be the people we are today. I think you're right. I have to say, with the exception of giving birth to my two children, I consider the day I met you as the beginning of my life, my real life. I never loved John the way I love you, Cal. Maybe that doesn't sound right, but it's true, nonetheless. He was my husband, but he wasn't my friend, lover, confidant, provider and soul mate like you are. I was married twice and neither one of them were there for me emotionally or physically. John was too busy working to have time for talking or making love and Derek was only interested in my money, not me. I totally understand what God meant when he said *two should become one.* I believe we are one person and always will be."

He leaned over and kissed her. "I feel the same way. We are one person; not because we never disagree, but because inside we think, feel and share everything. I did love Kathy and it was hard to go on after she died, but I don't think I would survive if something happened to you. Maybe that's why I always ask God, if it's his will, he would take us home at the same time."

"Now you're making me cry, Cal," Lucy said as she wiped the tears from her eyes. "Well, I'm not leaving this old world without you, either, so we might become immortal," she chuckled.

They were quiet for a while, each lost in thought.

Lucy asked, "How do you think Jarrod is doing with the horse you bought for him? He has quite an attachment to you, Cal. Ever since he first met you in Batavia, when Annie was in the hospital. He really wants to be a cowboy like his Grandpa Cal. That warms my heart."

Cal nodded and smiled. "When I'm with him, he seems to be a natural rider; more so than Doug, I believe. Doug is afraid and that makes him stiff and uncomfortable. You know, if we buy a horse for each of our grandchildren, we'll have to build a much bigger stable."

"I was thinking about that, too. They could share horses, of course. They probably won't all be there to ride at the same time, anyway. Gabe has attached himself to Nell and she is perfect therapy for him, plus the fact he doesn't deal well with change."

"We talked about letting the girls ride Harmony, but since she's due to foal in a few months, I don't think they should. Maybe we could buy the girls a horse and another for the boys. I know Jarrod will still have his, but he worked really hard for that horse and continues to take excellent care of him. Bethany doesn't want to ride any horse; she just wants to feed them." They both chuckled at that, knowing it was absolutely true.

Lucy smiled and commented, "If Ben and Candy continue to increase their family, they'll have to build the bigger stable and buy the horses. For right now, Luke is happy with his rocking horse."

Cal frowned a bit before continuing. "I was so pleased when Paul and Lynne agreed to move their family into the house on our second ranch. But now I really need to find a foreman for that ranch. I would rather select someone who already works for us than interview people. What are your thoughts on offering the job to Len? I know you two didn't get off to a very good start, but he is definitely qualified and I think he would be a good choice."

Lucy remembered the day she confronted Len when he told her she belonged in a kitchen and not on a cattle round-up. "I think he would do an excellent job. Did I ever tell you he came by after our competition and apologized for what he said and then congratulated me on finishing higher than him? I was extremely impressed by that. It takes a strong man to apologize. He has my vote."

"Good. I'll offer him the job when we get home; after I get Ben's input, of course."

* * *

"Dad, tell me everything you know about your father, okay?" Jarrod stood at Paul's desk with his pen and notebook in hand.

Paul glanced up from his paperwork and asked, "What are you working on, Jarrod?"

"Mom gave me an assignment for school and part of it is to write a report on my ancestors. I can wait until Grammy gets home to ask about her relatives, but I need you to tell me about your dad's side of the family now."

Paul leaned back in his desk chair. "I'm ashamed to say I don't know much about my father and I definitely don't know anything about his parents, my grandparents. We may have to ask your Grammy about him, too. She never talked about my dad's family and I was pretty young when he died. I don't remember meeting them...ever. That's sad, isn't it, Jarrod?"

Jarrod had a questioning look in his eyes. "Like... you mean, you never saw your grandparents? Really? I thought everyone had grandparents. Do you think Aunt Vicki would know something? I could look on the internet, I suppose. Mom isn't going to let me get by with saying, 'I couldn't find anything.'"

Paul laughed at his son. "Yeah, I see your dilemma. Mom's a tough teacher, huh? I will call Aunt Vicki and see if she's any more help than I am. See if your teacher will give you an extension on the due date of this assignment, okay?"

After Jarrod left the room, Paul called his sister, Victoria. "Vicki, this is Paul. Jarrod has an assignment to find information on his ancestry. He asked me about our dad and our grandparents. Do you remember anything?"

"No, unfortunately, I don't," Vicki answered. "We never heard from any grandparents that I remember; not even at Christmas or our birthdays. I guess we were pretty young when Dad got sick and we never asked. I think Mom may have some pictures from when we were little. She and Cal will be home tomorrow. Can it wait that long?"

"Yes, I'm sure it can. I'll persuade the teacher to grant an extension, since I know her pretty well," Paul replied. "By the way, how is Devon feeling? You told Lynne he had another urinary tract infection. Can't the medicines get it cleared up for good?"

Vicki sighed. "Yes, he does have another infection and believe it or not, he has high blood pressure. I didn't even know kids got high blood pressure. We have an appointment with a specialist next week. In the meantime, he is on prescriptions for both the infection and the blood pressure. I certainly hope they find the cause of these infections pretty soon."

"I'm sorry, Vicki. We will continue to pray about it. Is there anything else we can do for now?"

"I don't think so. I wish Mom was here. I know I like to complain about her 'take charge' attitude, but at this point, David and I would really welcome someone else to take charge for a while, y'know?"

Paul chuckled, "Yes, I know what you mean. I hope they enjoyed their two weeks of no problems or discussions because we already have some to hit them with when they get home."

CHAPTER 3

WHEN CAL AND LUCY PULLED INTO THE DRIVE in front of the house, Ben was on the front porch with Luke. The minute Luke saw Cal get out of the car, he wriggled off Ben's lap and ran to him with his arms up in the air.

"Hey Buddy, how's Grandpa's boy?" Cal asked him, as he hoisted Luke in the air before holding him on his arm and nuzzling his neck.

Luke was so happy to see them, he was spouting all sorts of gibberish instead of the words he knew. He used his chubby hand to turn Cal's face to him and planted a slobbery kiss on his cheek.

"That's the best welcome home anyone could ever give me," Cal said.

Candy heard Luke squealing and came out to see them, too. She looked uncomfortable but happy. Ben helped her to the swing and sat down beside her.

"How are you feeling, Candy?" Lucy asked.

"Like a whale," Candy replied. "And it's all your fault, Lucy."

Lucy laughed, "If I remember my procreation facts correctly, I believe you and Ben had something to do with this."

"Yes, I guess so. But you're the one who suggested we have a dozen."

"Guilty as charged," Lucy admitted. "At least you're having them two at a time so it won't take so long," she added.

Candy groaned and laughed at the same time. Ben put his arm around her shoulders and kissed the top of her head.

"You'll never guess what, Lucy," Candy said. "My mom and dad have been conversing with each other, apparently, and they're going to meet here before the babies are born. I'm kind of excited about that."

Lucy caught Cal's eye and said, "That sounds like a breakthrough, Candy. You've been praying for a long time they might be able to resolve their differences. Perhaps this is the beginning. But, I want you to know, we are not having a repeat of Luke's entry into the world. These babies are going to be born in a hospital or with a real midwife present, okay?"

"Aw, Lucy, you did as good a job of delivering Luke as any doctor or midwife could do," Ben told her.

"Thank you, but I would rather not repeat the experience," Lucy laughed.

Luke reached for Lucy, nearly falling out of Cal's arms. "Yeah, you missed your Grammy, too, didn't you, my little Luke?" Lucy said as she took him from Cal.

"We can talk more in the morning, but is there anything about the ranch I should know tonight?" Cal asked Ben.

"I sold the two matched geldings to the man from Bozeman, Montana. He contacted us several months ago, remember? He picked them up last week. He didn't argue about the price and paid in cash, which is sort of unusual, but I took it," Ben told Cal. "We talked for a while. He said he was a rodeo man and wanted to finish his career with the best horseflesh he could find. A friend of his recommended our stock. That makes me feel pretty good."

"Yes, that does feel good," Cal said. "I guess the Benson brand is getting some good exposure. I also want to talk to you about asking Len to be the second foreman, but it can wait until morning. It was a long flight and a wonderful two weeks but I think it's time for us to see the inside of our house, so we're going to say good night," Cal told them.

Lucy handed Luke back to Ben after she smothered him in kisses and went with Cal into their end of the huge ranch house.

Candy grinned at Ben and asked, "What do you suppose made them so tired?"

"Let's see...those two alone for two weeks with beautiful sun, sand and water and no phone calls or interruptions? I can't imagine," he laughed.

*   *   *

Jarrod was the first one to knock on the door in the morning while Cal and Lucy were eating breakfast. "Hi. I've brushed Caliper every day like you told me to, Grandpa, and I've cleaned his stall. Uncle Ben checked my saddle and everything before I rode him, too."

"It's nice to see you, Jarrod," Lucy told him when he took a breath. "Would you like some breakfast? And how did you get here every day?"

Ten-year-old Jarrod sat down at the table and drank a glass of juice. "I rode my bike today and I rode it here every day while you were gone. I have to do my schoolwork first but I hurry so I can come here to be with the horses."

Cal smiled at Lucy. "I think we have a *ranch man* in the making. He seems pretty dedicated. Does he remind you of anyone you know at this age?"

"Yes, he certainly does. The horses and roping and"...she stopped herself before she added poker and guns... "were all-consuming to me when I was his age."

She continued, "My advice to you, Jarrod? Don't leave Texas. Sometimes it takes a long time to find your way back."

Cal stood and kissed Lucy. "I'm going with Jarrod to see how well he's done, okay? Then maybe he and I will ride for a while. I'm anxious to get back on Cutter and Jarrod seems ready to go for a ride. How about it, Jarrod?"

"Yes, Sir, Grandpa. I'm ready and Caliper is, too. Let's go." He grabbed his hat and waited for Cal to put his on. They went out the door together. Lucy thought about how much she loved both of them.

After loading the dishwasher, she poured another cup of coffee and sat down to make a few calls. The first call was to her best friend, Phoebe.

"Phoebe? How are you? I know it's only been two weeks, but I wanted to check in with you. What's going on in your life?"

"Hi Lucy. First, tell me about your surprise get-away. Was it beautiful?"

"Oh my goodness, Phoebe. It was as close to heaven as a person can get while still here on earth. The sun shone every day, the water was the most beautiful shade of turquoise and as clear as glass, and the food was delicious. The activities available were pretty awesome, too. Maybe the best part was being isolated from everyone and everything for two weeks; just me and Cal...alone."

Phoebe chuckled, "I can see how that would be a great two weeks. I'm happy you had the opportunity to relax. I, on the other hand, have been working. I flew to Illinois for the official closing on the printing business and the house. While I was there, I stopped to see Anna again; you know, the girl who rents your building in Batavia and makes jewelry. I felt compelled to see her. Lucy, I am absolutely certain she is being abused by her husband, lover...whoever he is, but even though I hinted at it, she wouldn't open up about her situation. I didn't have any business cards with my new number on them, so I gave her one of yours, making the excuse that she might want to talk to you about buying the building. I hope that was okay."

"Yes, of course. Do you think she'll call if she's in trouble?" Lucy asked.

"I don't know. I really hope so. I'm not sure I know how to help her from a thousand miles away, but maybe I could convince her to seek some help and have some resources ready for her. I know from experience it is scary for her and I remember I didn't tell anyone, either."

When they finished visiting, Lucy called Vicki. Even though she called yesterday to let her know they were home, safe and sound, she didn't visit or ask about the children.

"Vicki, how is everyone at your house? I feel like I haven't seen the kids for a month instead of two weeks."

Vicki sighed, "Olivia has a cold, Bethany has been terrorizing everyone, as usual, and Devon is still not feeling good. His blood pressure is high and he has another urinary tract infection. We have an appointment with a specialist in Houston on Tuesday. David is going with me. Do you think you could watch Bethany and Olivia for the day?"

"Sure. That would be fine. If you have to leave early on Tuesday, you could bring them on Monday evening and they can stay the night," Lucy offered.

"Thanks, Mom. I appreciate it. I'm scared, truthfully. I want to know what's going on but part of me doesn't want to know."

"I can understand that, Vicki. But I think you will be relieved when you do know. You can't fight an enemy if you don't know who they are or what it is. Hang in there, Sweetie. God already knows what's going on. Trust him."

CHAPTER 4

"CORY, WOULD YOU PLEASE bring me the file folders of the two new men who came in a few days ago?" Leon asked the young man who would soon be leaving the men's residential rehab center in Loveland, Colorado.

"Sure thing, Mr. Henderson," Cory replied as he left to retrieve the files from the intake facilitator's office.

Leon watched him leave, and thought about Cory's journey. His was one of the many success stories Leon had witnessed in the years since he was hired as the administrator of Mountain House.

Leon reminisced a bit about how he first came as a resident but after turning his life around and earning his degree, he came back as a counselor and later, as the administrator. He could not make decisions as to who was accepted into the program *and* be their counselor, as that would be a conflict of interests, so there was an Acceptance Board. The members decided on the men who would be admitted into the program. Most of them were at the last stage before prison sentences. They had already been in enough trouble to warrant prison, but the overcrowded system made them one last offer to turn their lives around. There were a myriad of rules in place to keep them out of trouble while they lived there: no smoking, no drinking, no swearing, no weapons, no dating, and no free time outside the house. Since it was a Christian facility, weekly church attendance was a requirement, also.

They could work on getting their GEDs or if they had a high school diploma, they were encouraged to work on some higher education courses. Mountain House had classes for building a resume, interview skills, problem-solving and anger management. Those things all came *after* the men were clean and sober for a specified period of time.

Cory had achieved his goals and had a family support system to help him. He would be leaving soon and Leon was certain he would make it. Unfortunately, not all the men housed at Mountain House were successful in their bid to change their lives. If rules were broken, there were consequences. Some chose the consequences and opted out of staying there, which meant they were either immediately sentenced to prison or they were on the run.

"Here are the files you asked for, Mr. Henderson," Cory said as he placed them in Leon's outstretched hand. "I think I'm going to miss this place when I leave."

Leon smiled at him. "Yes, it is a bit of a scary time when you leave a safe place, but I have every confidence you will do fine, Cory."

After he closed the door behind him, Leon opened the two folders. *Nothing new,* he thought. *After a while, they all look the same. Different charges, different names and different home states but having no use for God in their lives was what made them their own worst enemy.* One of the files was considerably thicker than the other one. This man had been in and out of trouble so many times, he must have felt like he was on a merry-go-round. His offenses were many: drugs, public intoxication, robbery, domestic violence, and…weapon possession? Leon was surprised the Acceptance Board had approved him. Weapon possession was usually an automatic 'no' when they read through a file. Perhaps there was a reason for the exception. Leon would interview him later in the day and decide for himself. He did have the power to overturn a Board decision, but had only used it once.

Leon asked the first man to come into his office. There was no knock before the door was pushed open so hard it hit the wall behind it. He entered rather reluctantly as most of them did. They usually believed they would be psychoanalyzed again and the majority of them had been through some sort of questioning many times before.

"Hello, I'm Leon Henderson," he said as he shook hands with the tall, lanky, dark-haired man. "The first thing I want to ask you is please knock on doors before you go busting into a room, Okay?"

"Okay. It's a bad habit of mine, I guess," the young man acknowledged.

"You can relax. I'm not here to scold you or pick your brain, at least not today," Leon laughed. "I would like to know a little bit about you personally, aside from any charges on your record, okay?"

Warily, the young man nodded. "Okay, what do you want to know?"

"Let's start with, where you're from. Are you a native Coloradoan?"

"No. I've lived in so many states, I can't remember where my birth certificate says I was born."

"I understand that. Are your parents alive? Any siblings?"

"I never saw my old man. My mom died of a drug overdose when I was six or seven. Then I had a string of foster parents but I never got along much with any of them. I probably got a whole passel of half-brothers and sisters out there, but none I know of," he grinned. "As soon as I turned eighteen, I was on my own."

Leon nodded. "Have you ever been married?"

He shook his head. "No, I'm not that stupid. Shacked up with a girl for a while, but she left when she found out she was pregnant, but she didn't tell me. Do you mind if I stand instead of sitting in a chair?"

"Go right ahead."

He stood and looked out the window for a bit, then turned and looked at the family photos on the bookshelves. "One of these your wife, Mr. Henderson?"

"Yes, the one on the right. The other one is my sister and the third one is my son and his wife. He works here too and I'm sure you'll meet him soon."

He picked up the picture of Leon's sister, Lucy, and scrutinized it.

"Is something wrong?" Leon asked.

"No. She looks like someone I should know but I don't hardly think I'd know your sister, would I?"

"That would be unlikely, especially since she lives in Texas. One more question for today. You said your girlfriend was pregnant; did you ever see the child?"

There was a long pause. "Yeah, there were two of them and I saw 'em but they ain't my kids any more. I signed 'em away."

Leon sensed an acute sadness in this young man. As he turned to go, Leon held out his hand and said, "I'm happy you're here...even if *you* aren't too thrilled about it at this point. We'll talk again, Blake Tanner."

CHAPTER 5

"MOM ASKED US TO COME FOR DINNER on Monday evening when we take Olivia and Bethany to stay the night. Is that okay with you, David?" Vicki asked.

"Sure," David answered. Then he laughed, "Did she say what was on the menu? You know she doesn't like to cook." He was thoughtful for a minute. "Isn't it strange that a woman who admits she doesn't like to cook and says she isn't very good at it, managed to fix meals for 30 ranch hands for an entire week when Dolores had to leave?"

Vicki nodded. "Yes, she did. First of all, she is much better at cooking than she admits and she did it because Cal needed her to do it, plain and simple."

"Don't forget the incentive of a $20,000 cutting horse she wanted," David reminded her.

"Yes, but I know she would have done it for him without the 'bonus' of the horse. She would do anything for Cal, I believe. And he would move heaven and earth for her."

David nodded. "They do have something special, don't they? Just like us, Vicki," he said as he swept her into his arms and kissed her.

When he let her go and she caught her breath, she told him, "Wow. I know there was something I wanted to tell you, but that kiss just made me forget what it was."

David laughed at her. "You were talking about going to your mom's for dinner."

"That's right," Vicki remembered. "Paul and Lynne and the kids will be there, too. It seems Lynne assigned Jarrod a school project about ancestors. Paul couldn't help him with any information about our father and I couldn't either. I think Mom has some pictures she wants to give us. Maybe that will shed some light on the subject."

* * *

Lucy fingered the old snapshots she had in a box. There weren't too many, but Paul and Vicki should have them. She planned to give them to the two of them tonight after dinner. Jarrod's school project had certainly brought a lot of memories and emotions back to the surface. Maybe that's why the photos were in a box buried deep in the back of the closet. Even though she had forgiven John for many things, real or perceived, she obviously still had a lot of feelings buried along with the photos. The unbidden tears rolled down her cheeks...so long ago, so unnecessary. *Oh John, what happened to the college boy I fell in love with?*

That's how Cal found her...on the couch, with the box on her lap and tears slipping silently down her cheeks.

"Lucy? What's wrong?" He sat next to her and put his arm around her. "What can I do, Sweetheart?"

"Nothing." She shook her head. "This will be my story to tell tonight, but I would like you to be with me when I do. I don't know how much Vicki and Paul actually remember about John. I tried to shield them from a lot when he was sick but we all know, kids see and hear much more than we think they do. I know Vicki has always sensed my anger toward her father but we've never discussed it. I remember saying it was time to forgive him at the same time I forgave Leon for selling the Yellow Rose."

"I'll be right by you, Lucy. Do they know about the trust he set up and the trial you were involved in years later, because of that trust?"

"Paul, of course, knows about a trial because he and Lynne lived just a few blocks from me and at one point in time, it was spread all over the newspapers, but he never asked about it or about my involvement in it. I don't know if he didn't want to know or was too busy to read about it."

She took a deep breath. "I will tell Jarrod what he wants to know and then tell Paul and Victoria the rest of the story after the kids leave the room. I want the grandchildren to have only good things in their memory banks about their grandfather and the pictures will help with that."

"Maybe you shouldn't tell Paul and Vicki any more than you tell Jarrod. What difference does it make after all these years? It will only hurt them and their memories of their father. What good will it do to hash over all the bad stuff again?"

Lucy looked at him for a bit and wiped her tears. "As usual, you're right, Cal. I'm telling them to make *me* feel better but it will tarnish their vision of John. That isn't fair to them or to him. I will tell them about his good qualities and why I was attracted to him in the first place."

With six adults and five children eating, dinner was a noisy affair. After the table was cleared, Lucy emptied the box of photographs onto it. She spread them out so everyone could see them.

"I didn't remember my father was so tall," Paul said as he picked up a picture of John and Lucy standing together at the ranch house before they were married.

Lucy glanced at Cal and smiled, "Yes, I've always had a weakness for tall men."

Jarrod had his notebook ready. "Okay, Grammy, tell me about my grandfather and his parents."

Lucy placed her arm around his shoulders. "I'm sorry to say there isn't much to tell, Jarrod. I met your grandfather, John, when we were in college together. He was a good-looking, smart young man and I fell head over heels in love with him. When I asked to meet his parents, he told me he didn't have any. I felt a kinship, I guess, because I didn't have any, either. We were both orphans, but in different ways. I remembered my parents but he was placed for adoption as soon as he was born. He lived in an orphanage for a while, but then it was a series of foster homes. Even though life wasn't so good for him, he always made sure he got good grades in school. When he graduated at the top of his high school class, he had earned a scholarship to college. All he ever wanted to do was paint cars or trucks or any kind of vehicle and he was excellent at it. People would bring their cars from far away to have John Newsome re-paint them."

She picked up several pictures of John standing by a car he had finished painting. "See that one? I remember it was some important racing car from Georgia."

Jarrod looked at the pictures and then closed his notebook. "I don't know what to write, Mom. Grandpa didn't have any family before him, so I guess he is the first generation and Dad is the second and I'm the third. We'll have to keep going forward because there isn't any history going backward."

Lynne hugged him. "It's okay, Jarrod. Sometimes, that's the way life is. I know it's hard for you and Annie to think your Dad didn't ever have any grandparents, but God has blessed *you* with some. You have Grammy and Grandpa Cal and besides, ancestors aren't always related by blood. The best kind of relatives are connected to us by love."

Devon and Bethany and Annie were looking at the pictures, too. "Is that you, Grammy?" Devon asked.

"Yep, that's me, and that baby is your mother. The little boy is Uncle Paul."

Bethany thought seeing Vicki as a baby was pretty funny. "You and mommy look different, Grammy."

Lucy laughed and said, "That's what getting older does to you, Bethany; you look different than when you were young."

Lucy handed Jarrod a piece of paper with a list of birth and death dates of her parents and grandparents and even great-grandparents. "Maybe this will give you something to research on my side of the family, Jarrod. If you look back far enough, you'll find that Grandpa Cal and I share a few relatives."

Devon was still looking at photos with a concerned look on his face. "So...Mom, your dad didn't have any parents just like me and Bethany, right? Only we got you and Dad now, but he never was adopted, right?"

'That's right, Devon. He wasn't adopted when he was a child."

"That's sad," Devon said. He put his arms around David's neck and declared, "I'm sure glad we belong to you and Mom."

All the adults in the room were nearly in tears. "I'm sure glad, too, Devon," David whispered to him.

When the older children went to the great room to watch a movie, Paul asked Lucy, "I sense there are things about our father that you didn't want to share with Jarrod, Mom. Is that true?"

"Only a few, Paul." She looked at Cal for support. He took her hand and she continued, "Everything I said about him was true. He was a good man. He picked up some bad habits and bad friends when he was growing up without any guidance, but he managed to overcome most of them. I think his 'bad boy' image is what drew me to him in the first place. I'm not going to go into detail about our lives, but there are a few things you should know, I think."

Lucy continued, "He loved you and Vicki and me, but his idea of showing us that love was to make as much money as he could and provide for us. That wouldn't be a bad thing if he could have balanced working and being at home, too. He couldn't, and that's why you have no recollections of him reading you a story or playing catch in the yard or even the four of us eating together as a family very often. He worked all the time. We lacked his emotional and physical presence."

"He was also a very stubborn man. When he started painting, of course, there were no OSHA rules or big filtering masks and suits to wear, but even later, when they *were* required, he refused to use them. It's sort of like people who refuse to wear seat belts because they believe nothing will ever happen to them. John breathed so many fumes and overspray in his lifetime, I'm surprised he didn't die sooner than he did."

Lucy turned to her daughter and continued, "Vicki, you asked me once if I was angry with your dad. Yes, I was. He may have died of lung cancer anyway, but not nearly as soon as he did. His refusal to try to protect himself seemed like a form of suicide to me. It told me we weren't important enough to live for. He realized that before he died. As he became sicker, he drew closer to the Lord and ironically, I moved further away from the Lord. I couldn't forgive him for a long time and blamed every bad thing in our lives on him, but that isn't true any longer.

When I met and fell in love with Cal, he made me realize if I wanted to claim Christ's forgiveness for my sins, I needed to be willing to forgive, also. That meant your Uncle Leon and your father. If there's anything I want you to take away from this conversation, it is this: I am so very, very grateful for God's leading the two of you to the life mates you have and for keeping you anchored to him even through a difficult childhood and through my unbelief. I also see you spending time with your spouses and children and that is way more important than money. If your father were here, he would agree with that so let's allow that to be his legacy to you, okay?"

By this time, she had tears in her eyes again. Cal put her head on his shoulder and dried them. Vicki and David and Paul and Lynne sat quietly for a while, each lost in their own thoughts. Finally, Paul spoke, "Mom, I think I can speak for Vicki and me when I say you did an amazing job as a single mother. I honestly don't remember feeling like we lacked anything, except Dad, of course. I don't want you to have any regrets, either. Enjoy your life with Cal and make up for the years you were alone. God has indeed blessed all of us and we need to be thankful for those blessings."

Chapter 6

"WHAT AM I GOING TO DO, SANDI? I can see it now; I'll be one of the homeless people living in a cardboard box under a bridge," the woman sitting across from her whined.

"Come on, Tess, don't talk that way. You still have your apartment," Sandi told her.

"I won't have it for more than a few months. Then I'll run out of money and won't be able to pay the rent. I won't be able to come see you, either, after my insurance runs out and I don't know how to function without talking to my therapist," she cried into a tissue.

"Tell me exactly what happened, Tess," Sandi encouraged her.

"The company I've worked for was absorbed by a conglomerate. They promised they would keep all the employees and train them for new positions. But as soon as the deal was finalized, they down-sized and any of us who were over fifty-five years old, were terminated. No warning, no letters of recommendation, very little compensation and our insurance is only good for three months."

"Okay, Tess, let's break this down into possibilities. Do you have any savings or stock or a 401K you can use to stay afloat for a while?"

"I've never been very good at saving money. I spend way too much; I know that. Once upon a time, I had lots of money. My father left me half of a ranch in Texas when he died. My brother bought my half and I had a bundle." She started crying again. "But I went through that like the people who win the lottery and are broke in a year. I spent all of it."

Sandi tried another tactic. "So, you have a brother, in Texas. Could you ask him for help or perhaps go there to live until you can get back on your feet?"

Tess' eyes got as big as saucers. "Never … never would I ask Calvin for help. No. Never. No, no, no."

"Why not? That's what families are for, to support each other. Is he not a nice person?"

Tess sighed and grabbed another tissue. "I couldn't really tell you if he's a nice person or not. I haven't seen him for many, many years. I didn't go to the funeral when his first wife died. I didn't go to his wedding when he remarried a few years ago. I never wrote, sent cards to his kids or anything. I have no contact with him and of all the places on earth I could live, it would not be Texas. My mother hated Texas and divorced my dad to move back to civilization and I wouldn't go back."

"How old were you when your mother moved you away from Texas, Tess?"

"I don't know. Maybe two or three."

"Then how do you know you wouldn't like it? You're adopting your mother's attitude about something you know nothing about."

"I won't contact my brother and that's that," Tess said defiantly.

"Okay, then I suggest you send as many resumes as you possibly can, attend job fairs and consider selling some of your possessions until you find another job. I'll see you next week and we'll discuss how you're doing, okay?"

Tess nodded. She left Sandi's office and hailed a cab. When she thought about how she would be walking instead of riding in a cab when her last bit of savings was gone, she started to cry all over again. She would do anything before she called her brother.

*   *   *

"Bethany, what have you been eating?" Cal asked as she kissed him on the cheek.

"A strawberry popsicle, Grandpa. Are my lips cold?"

"Yes, they are cold and quite sticky," he laughed.

"Grammy ate one, too. I bet her lips are cold and sticky, just like mine."

"I think I'll find out," Cal said as he kissed Lucy. "Mmmm, strawberry kisses. My favorite."

Bethany giggled. "I think Grammy likes it when you kiss her, Grandpa. She's smiling."

"Bethany, you're pretty perceptive for a four-year-old," Lucy told her.

"What's *ceptive* mean, Grandpa?"

"It means you know a lot of things, Bethany and you're right about Grammy smiling," Cal told her.

"This is an awfully long conversation about a popsicle," Lucy laughed.

"Do you know when David and Vicki will be home or will they stay in Houston tonight?" Cal asked her.

"I'm expecting them today, unless there are tests that can't be completed in one day. I'm sure Vicki would call if they were going to stay. I hear Olivia. Will you keep an eye on Bethany while I get her?" Lucy asked Cal.

"Sure. Bethany and I just might eat another popsicle. It's pretty hot outside. We need to cool down, don't we, Sweetie?"

When Lucy returned with Olivia, she placed her in her booster seat at the table so she could have a snack. Bethany immediately started sharing her popsicle with Olivia.

"Cal," Lucy said. "Stop her. I'm pretty sure neither one of them is supposed to have anything with red dye in it, but especially Olivia because she's younger. Heaven help us. You can't take your eyes off Bethany for a second, okay?"

Cal started laughing. "Calm down, Grammy. I've got this. Come on Bethany, let's wash you up and then we'll go outside so we don't get in any more trouble. Okay?" He winked at Lucy as he took Bethany to the sink to wash her hands and face.

'I'm getting too old for this. I can definitely take care of them, but I can't keep up with all the rules about what they can and can't eat,' Lucy decided. She gave Olivia some Goldfish crackers, knowing they were on the approved list of snacks. She should never have given Bethany the red popsicle to begin with. *I wonder how many red things my kids ate before we knew anything about dyes and allergies and behaviors,* she thought.

While she was chastising herself, David called to say they would be home in a few hours.

"Can you tell me briefly what the doctors said?" Lucy asked.

"No, it's too complicated, but it definitely isn't good and Vicki isn't dealing with it too well. We'll see you in a little while."

Lucy watched Olivia eat crackers. She was such a pretty little girl, with her dark curls, dark eyes and pink cheeks and an ever-present smile. *'Heavenly Father, I don't know what is in store for Devon but please calm Vicki and David so they remember you are in charge and keep Bethany and Olivia in your safe embrace also,'* she prayed.

* * *

Bethany and Cal were back in the house when David, Vicki and Devon returned. Devon seemed undaunted by his day of being poked and tested.

"Grammy, you should see this really cool machine the doctor had. It looked like a spaceship."

"Really, Devon? I'm glad you had an interesting day," Lucy said as she looked at Vicki questioningly. Vicki shook her head; she looked exhausted and defeated.

Ben had obviously seen them drive in and came to take Devon and Bethany to his house while the adults discussed the diagnosis.

"Hey, kids, why don't we go to my house? I think Aunt Candy is dishing up ice cream," Ben told them. They raced each other to the door and couldn't get out fast enough.

Cal poured coffee for David and Vicki. Lucy took Vicki's hand. "So tell us what you found out today, Sweetheart."

Vicki looked at David. "I'll let David tell you because I can't. I'll cry and not be able to speak. I've held my tears all day for Devon's sake, but I can't any longer."

David told them, "The doctor, a nephrologist, wanted a blood sample, a urine sample and an imaging test of the kidneys. He asked a million questions about family health history, which is nearly non-existent in Devon's case. I was impressed with Devon, though. He thought peeing in a cup was funny and he did very well with the blood draw. The spaceship he was talking about houses an MRI for children. They took images of his kidneys and he stayed perfectly still. He really was a trooper through all of it."

"He has many of the symptoms the doctor was listing. His growth rate has slowed, he has the chronic urinary tract infections and he has been unusually tired," Vicki added. "Plus, he has high blood pressure."

Cal asked, "What are the suggestions they're giving you to cure this?"

"That's just it...there is no cure. Chronic kidney disease is something that doesn't go away. He will have to take antibiotics for the infections, we'll have to monitor what he eats and he'll also need medicine to lower the high blood pressure," David told them. "We received much more information about the type of kidney disease he has and lots of big words and terms but it all boils down to the fact he will eventually need a transplant."

"Yes, the medications will merely keep it at bay. The only options are dialysis or a transplant." Vicki could hardly say the words. She put her head down on the table and sobbed.

David placed his arms around her and pulled her head onto his shoulder. "We'll get through this, Honey. Devon's a strong kid. There will be a donor, I'm sure."

Lucy was trying to absorb all the information. "How do you go about finding a donor? Does it have to be a child donor?"

"No. In fact, a kidney from an adult is preferred. If there could be one from a close living relative, that's the best scenario, but if that can't happen, his name will go onto a national donor list and we wait until one is available. I don't know how we'll get one from either of his parents and that's the only biological adult relatives he has," David said.

Lucy asked, "Can't the adoption agency find his birth mother for you? I mean, they should know if she's still in prison or not. And don't you have his father's address? You send pictures once in a while, right?"

Vicki shook her head. "For the last year or more, any pictures we sent to the address he gave us are returned because he doesn't live there any longer. We stopped sending anything."

Vicki shook her head. "I'm really, really frightened, Mom. What if a donor is never found? What if…" She started to cry again and could not finish the thought.

"I don't see that we can accomplish anything tonight," Cal interjected. "I propose we pray about this and place it in God's hands. In the morning, when you aren't exhausted and can think clearly again, you can check with the adoption agency or the prison to see if you can find the mother's whereabouts. I think she's your best bet because finding the father will be virtually impossible."

They held hands while Cal prayed, "Father, we come to you to ask your protection and healing for Devon and for peace for David and Victoria. Help them to know your comfort and feel your presence in this situation. We don't know the plans you have for their lives but we trust your goodness and love for all of us. If it is your will, let a donor be found so Devon can return to a normal life. We ask these things in Jesus' name. Amen."

Vicki stood and said she was going to get Bethany and Devon. Lucy went to pack Olivia's things and David thanked Cal for everything.

"David, I'm not minimizing *your* fears and concerns, but it always seems emotionally rougher for moms, so stay close to Vicki, okay?" Cal advised him.

David nodded, "I will, for sure."

As Cal and Lucy lay in bed, Lucy said, "You know, since both parents have records with the law *and* they have felonies, they have to be in the system somewhere. I realize it may not be public information but I'm pretty certain I know someone who can get that information for me. I think I may be able to find Mr. Blake Tanner."

Cal smiled at her. "Now, how did I know that was exactly what you were going to say, Lucy?"

"Because you know me so well, Cowboy," she laughed.

CHAPTER 7

LEON CALLED BRUCE HALLOWAY into his office. "Hello Bruce. Have a seat."

The barrel-chested man slumped into a chair, without returning the greeting.

"I want to ask you a few questions about your personal life, Bruce, just to get to know you a little better."

"Why? You don't need to know me any better. I'm here against my will."

"You aren't being forced to stay here, Bruce. You can leave any time you want," Leon reminded him.

"Yeah, right," Bruce sneered. "If I leave this prison, I'll be sentenced to another one."

"I prefer to think Mountain House is much better than being in prison, Bruce. You can acquire some life skills and disciplines so you won't be in this situation again."

"Don't kid yourself, old man. I won't be here long. You got more rules than a warden. And that going to church on Sundays? What a joke."

"You should try it, Bruce. You never know what may happen to your heart when you hear God's word."

Bruce shook his head and dropped his eyes to look at the floor.

"Do you have any siblings, Bruce? Are your parents still alive?"

Bruce sat with his hands folded in his lap but wouldn't answer any of Leon's questions.

"Okay, that's all for today. Maybe you'll feel like talking after you've been here for a few weeks. You can go, Bruce. Enjoy the rest of your day, if you can."

Leon walked down the hall to his son's office. Seeing the door ajar, he knocked softly. When Clint saw him, he motioned for him to come inside.

"How is Janet feeling?" was Leon's first question.

Clint grinned. "I think she feels great, but she might tell you otherwise. Just thinking about being a father gives me goosebumps, even though it's a long way off."

"Thinking about being a grandfather gives *me* goosebumps," Leon laughed. "I haven't called Lucy and Cal yet, but I know they will be thrilled for the two of you."

"Did you want to talk about one of the newly admitted men?"

"Yes, actually, both of them. From my preliminary observations, I believe Blake Tanner will be okay. He's already been clean for several months. He was picked up on an old warrant and the judge sent him here because he thought Blake would have a chance at total rehabilitation here rather than prison.

"The other man, Bruce Halloway, has a chip on his shoulder the size of Nebraska. He seems potentially violent to me, but I've only seen him for a few unproductive minutes. Perhaps you will see another side of him. I hope so. I saw he had some weapons charges in his file. I know we search all bags and backpacks when the men return from somewhere, but I'm wondering if it would be a good idea to institute a new policy of patting them down for any concealed weapons, also."

Clint thought about that for a minute. "I think it would probably be a good idea. You must really be having some bad vibes about this guy."

Leon shook his head. "I'm not sure what it is exactly. I've seen lots of men come in here with a bad attitude, but this one seems different...lots of anger under the surface. I don't want to write him off so soon. After all, we're here to help these men. Fortunately, God doesn't write us off, so Bruce deserves a chance like everyone else here. We'll see what happens in the next few weeks."

* * *

Tess sat in Sandi's office looking proud of herself. She had a notebook in her hands.

"Okay, Tess, tell me how you're doing. Have you sent any resumes? Looked for a less expensive apartment?"

Tess nodded. "Yes, I sent resumes and I applied at a temp agency, but I haven't heard anything from any of them. I brought a list of the places I applied. I also have a list of the antiques and valuables I want to sell." She handed the notebook to Sandi.

"I'm impressed, Tess. You've done some work here. It appears you've come to grips with the fact you might have to make some changes. Have you contacted your brother yet?"

Tess shook her head. "No. I do not want to call him. I'm sure one of these companies will call me and everything will be back to normal."

"I certainly hope so. We'll think positive. I think you should at least make contact with your brother and his family. You don't have to ask for help, just make it a friendly letter. Then if...and I said if...you would need his help, it wouldn't be quite as awkward."

"I'll think about it," Tess said. "I don't even know if he lives on the same ranch."

Sandi laughed. "That's what return address labels are for, Tess. If the address is wrong, it will come back to you."

"Yeah, I suppose. I'll send something this week...maybe."

*   *   *

When Tess entered her apartment, she considered Sandi's advice. It probably wouldn't hurt anything to send Cal a letter. *How long had it been? Fifteen years? Maybe twenty or thirty.* Tess wondered what he looked like now that he was older. He was always a very handsome young man.

She sat at her computer and typed a short note. When it was printed, she re-read it.

Hello Calvin,

It's been a long time since you've heard from me. I apologize for that and for not coming to Kathy's funeral or your wedding, a few years ago.

I really have no excuse other than I've been very busy and time seems to slip by.

I wanted to reconnect and let you know I'm still alive and I continue to live in New York. I hope all is well with you and your family.

Your sister, Tess

It didn't say what she really wanted to tell him, but it was a start. Hopefully, she wouldn't have to write another one, begging for his help.

She sealed it into an envelope and put a stamp on it. She paused as she wrote the address of the ranch where she thought he still lived, and then added her return address. She decided not to send it immediately, but to think about it for a few more days.

*   *   *

"How's your search for Blake Tanner going, Lucy?" Cal asked.

"Not so well, unfortunately. The person who is working on this tells me he has probably used some aliases, but there is no paper trail for the last six months to a year. He hasn't used a credit card, hasn't signed anything and obviously has stayed out of trouble, because the only thing on record besides his previous felonies, is an old warrant that no one has picked him up for."

"There are no addresses, either?" Cal questioned.

"There was one, but he was no longer there. Now he seems to have dropped off the face of the earth; there is no address. I don't know how he's living without an address of some sort. It's impossible to apply for help or a job without an address. Maybe he's joined the throngs of homeless people or…oh, Cal, what if he's dead?"

Lucy didn't want to consider that possibility. Blake Tanner had to be out there somewhere and she needed to find him.

"Has Vicki said if they found Devon's mother? Is she still in prison?"

"Yes, she is still serving her time. I don't know if she's been approached about being a donor. There are so many legalities and restrictions when looking for possible donor candidates. It's frustrating."

Cal poured himself another cup of coffee. "Ben told me Candy received a call from her father. It seems he and her mother, Myrna, want to come here for a few days and talk to them about something important. I wish it was to tell them they were getting remarried to each other, but you and I know that's not why they're coming. They have obviously decided to tell Candy about her childhood and that Myrna is not her birth mother. Do you have Myrna's number? I want to let her know I'm going to tell Ben about this before they get here."

Lucy checked her contact list and gave him the number. "What's your plan if she says you can't tell him?" Lucy asked.

Cal thought for a minute. "Then I'm going to do something I don't think I've ever done; I'm going to break a confidence and tell him anyway. He's my son and I love Candy as my daughter. I don't care that they are adults and can handle their own affairs. I'm not going to stand by and allow something hurtful destroy their lives."

Lucy nodded. "I completely agree with you and I'll go with you when you talk to Ben if you want me or I'll let you handle it by yourself."

* * *

"I think our prayers may take us until noon today," Cal said. "Let's walk while we pray... there will be fewer distractions that way."

Lucy thought she might have to pinch herself. If anyone had told her, several years ago when she was running her business in Chicago, that one day she would be going for a morning walk with a tall, handsome man who loved her unconditionally and saying prayers with him, she would have accused them of being either drunk or high or just plain delirious.

Before they started their walk, Cal told her, "By the way, the leader of the praise team at church asked me if I would consider substituting for their guitar player who had an emergency appendectomy and is having some complications. What do you think?"

Lucy smiled at him. "Go for it, Cal. You're certainly good enough and I think it would be good for you to have an audience besides me and an entire roomful of grandchildren."

CHAPTER 8

PHOEBE AND LUCY SAT ON OPPOSITE SIDES of a booth at an ice cream shop in Cypress and shared a huge chocolate sundae.

"This was a great idea, Phoebe," Lucy said between mouthfuls of ice cream dripping with chocolate sauce and whipped cream. "We can each feel less guilty about eating the entire thing."

Phoebe nodded. "We used to share food all the time when we went out together in Illinois. Does that seem like another lifetime, Lucy?"

"Yes, my friend, it certainly does. It's funny you would say that because I was thinking that very thing when Cal and I went walking and praying the other morning. Even after almost three years of loving that man, I sometimes think I will wake up one day and it will all have been a dream. Most of it a very pleasant dream," she chuckled, "but a dream, nonetheless."

"I don't know about you, but if it's a dream, I'm praying I never wake up," Phoebe stated.

"Are you and Jerry going to be in church on Sunday? Cal is playing with the praise team. I think he's a little nervous. This man who faces ornery horses and mean cattle and some crazy ranch hands and who lives with *me*...is nervous. Go figure."

Phoebe laughed at the picture Lucy painted. "We'll be sure to be there. You know, Lucy, speaking of church...I believe

I've accepted the fact that God has forgiven me for my past sins. I'm probably still not to the point where I talk to him about everything, as you and Cal do, or have the relationship with him that I want to have, but I do pray with Jerry when he prays and we discuss a lot of spiritual things."

"We share so many life experiences, Phoebe. We both fell in love with godly men who through their actions and prayers have led us to Christ. What better trait to look for in a man? Although I certainly wasn't looking for that. I simply fell in love with the way my cowboy *looked* when I first saw him," Lucy laughed.

"Have you thought about what you might get Cal for his birthday this year?"

"I can't think of anything. The man needs nothing and when it comes to clothing or boots or hats...I would never choose those for him. I considered one of the BBQ guns, and Ben told me he does look at a particular saddle every time they are in the western store."

"Forgive my ignorance, but what the heck is a BBQ gun? Do they use them to light the grill?"

They both laughed out loud. "That's a good one, Phoebe. They are special edition pistols with fancy designs on them. Kimber, a gun manufacturer puts out new editions each summer. They are beautiful, but a man's gun is a very personal thing and I would want Cal to choose his own. Maybe after he chooses it, I will pay for it. I don't know; I guess I'll think about it a little more."

A frown appeared on Phoebe's face. "Have Vicki and David heard any more about a kidney donor?"

"They've heard that the mother had some childhood disease which rules her out as a donor. I still haven't found the father but that doesn't mean he's not out there somewhere. His name will show up eventually. That's something we *definitely* pray about every day." After a few minutes, she continued, "You haven't said anything about the clothing shop for abused women. How's that project progressing?"

"It's coming along. The shelter in Magnolia gave me a room to use for the donations. In exchange for the space, Jerry has agreed to do some pro bono legal work for any women who need it. Right now, it's mostly organizing and sorting through the things that have come in. It amazes me what some people donate, and I don't mean that in a good way. There are some things that are dirty, need repairs or are really inappropriate clothing for *anyone* to wear, let alone a woman who might need to look presentable for a job interview or something similar."

"Can I help, Phoebe?" Lucy asked.

"I would love for you to come and see the place and give me some suggestions. It's hard for me, emotionally; to see these women who are in the same position I was in many years ago. I see the haunted look in their eyes, and I'm reminded of my life for so many years..." her voice trailed off as she looked out the window.

Lucy reached across the table and took her hand. "I know, Phoebe. It has to be hard; I'm sure the memories come flooding back. Please know that you are in my prayers, too. I also thank God you now have a good man who loves you."

Lucy gathered her things. "I'll call and we'll find a time to meet at the shop. Right now, I have to get home. Sean is dropping Doug and Amy off on his way to some meeting in Tomball, and Annie and Jarrod are riding their bikes over. The girls are going to bake cookies while Doug and Jarrod go riding." Lucy made a face about the cookie baking.

Phoebe laughed at her. "I thought you liked to bake cookies with your grandchildren."

"I do, but I thought I might be reaching the end of the cookie baking, but now there's Bethany and Olivia coming along and we don't know what the twins' gender is yet. I envision myself baking cookies until I'm ninety."

"Since I don't have any grandchildren, you'll have to tell me why it is so much better to bake cookies with Grammy than with Mom."

"That's easy. Grammy doesn't get upset about spilled flour and sugar and some pieces of eggshells in the dough. Mommies tend to fuss about messes more than I do. When Vicki was little, I fussed about spills too, but now, it doesn't seem so important any more. I guess that is called 'age perspective.'"

*   *   *

"Ben, I would like to talk to you about something. Can we go riding? I do my best thinking on horseback," Cal laughed.

"Sure. Although the last time we had a really serious talk while riding, you told me to ask Candy to marry me, I believe. I took your advice, so what's this about?" Ben asked.

Cal pulled on the brim of his hat and cleared his throat. "I don't know where to start exactly. When Frank and Myrna were here the first time, when Luke was born, Myrna shared something with Lucy. She told Myrna that we have no secrets, so she would have to tell me and Myrna was okay with that. We have kept that secret because we didn't know if it would ever be shared by Candy's parents or not, so there was no reason to tell. However, now they are coming to visit, but also, specifically to tell Candy something they should have told her twenty years ago. I have their permission to tell you because you're going to have to be her support and protector more than you have ever been before."

Ben's face registered his confusion and his anger and he had not heard the facts yet.

"Okay, I can't imagine what it is, but if it's going to harm Candy in some way, I will not allow it," Ben said.

Cal looked at his son, and thought what a good man he was. "You know that Candy has always said her mother was unkind to her and her father did almost all of the nurturing and taking care of her when she was a child. The reason for that is because Myrna is not Candy's mother. Frank had an affair with a young woman who became pregnant but died giving birth to Candy. He begged Myrna to take him and the baby back into their family. She did, but by her own admission, she never forgave him and took all her hateful feelings out on Candy."

Ben stopped riding and looked at Cal in disbelief. "You have got to be kidding me. They haven't told her in all these years and now, when she's happy and has a family of her own, they feel the need to confess? They still don't care about Candy. They just want to assuage their own consciences to make themselves feel better."

"Perhaps you're right, Ben. I don't know why they're feeling the need to tell her, but I do know she will feel betrayed, hurt and angry; every emotion you can think of and I wanted you to be prepared so you can assure her you are the one solid thing in her life and you will always be there for her. I realize she already knows that but you may have to reassure her ten times a day."

"I'm having a hard time wrapping my head around this, Dad. I want to go home and tell Candy so I can hold her and love her while she tries to absorb it and then I want to tell them they aren't welcome here."

Cal nodded. "I know, Son. I understand your feelings and I personally have no problem with you telling her, but I wouldn't do it today. I advise you to think about it and pray for wisdom for a few days. Then follow your heart about how to handle the whole mess with the least residual fallout and the least harm to Candy. *She's* your first priority, not her parents."

CHAPTER 9

WHEN ANNIE CAME IN THE DOOR, she handed Lucy a letter. "Mom says this came to our house but it's addressed to Grandpa."

"Okay, Sweetie, put it on the desk and I'll tell him when he comes in, okay?"

Lucy and the girls started on the cookies, while Jarrod and Doug went to find Cal in the office at the end of the stables. Jarrod always did an excellent job of saddling his horse and helping Doug with his, but the rule was that they couldn't ride until an adult checked everything first.

After a few hours, the entire house smelled like freshly baked cookies and the boys returned from their ride. Before they finished brushing their horses down, Cal told them to get Lucy, quickly.

"Grammy, you're supposed to come to the stables right now and Grandpa Cal says to bring the girls if you want them to have an education… whatever that means," Doug added.

"Come on, girls," Lucy said as she washed her hands. "I think I'm going to be a grandma again, but this time to a horse."

Harmony was indeed in labor. Cal let the children watch over the top of the stall door, while Lucy went in and knelt down by Harmony's head.

Amy asked Cal, "Aren't you going in the stall to help Grammy?"

"No, Amy. We'll stay out here...the fewer people in there, the better. We don't want to upset Harmony. It may take a while for her to have her baby and we don't want to make her nervous. Besides, your Grammy knows what she's doing. She probably helped her grandfather deliver babies when she was your age."

"Really?" Amy asked. All four of the children looked at Cal as though they didn't believe him.

"It's okay, Baby. You can do this; I know you can. Relax and it will go so much faster." She stroked Harmony's neck and continued to talk to her. Lucy remembered being with her grandpa countless times as horses gave birth. Most of the time, they accomplished it with no help at all, but when a mare needed assistance, he always had Lucy do it because she had smaller hands and arms and wouldn't harm the mare.

"I really thought it would be a few more days," she said to Cal. "She didn't show the usual signs but I'm glad we moved her to the stall with the clean straw last night." Lucy sat down in the straw next to Harmony's head. She talked to her for what seemed like hours.

As Harmony strained, the children were fascinated. When a tiny hoof appeared, Cal told Lucy, "You may have to reach in to straighten the other leg; I see only one."

She washed and lubricated her arm to reach inside Harmony. She followed the leg that was protruding until she found the other one and straightened it so both hooves would deliver at the same time. After that, it wasn't long until the entire foal was out. Harmony and the foal rested for a bit. Harmony stood and the foal attempted to stand but was still too new and wobbly.

Lucy had forgotten there was an audience of children watching. When she looked at them, their eyes were huge and they were all speechless; a rare occurrence.

"You did a good job, Harmony," Lucy told her mare. "Especially for a first time momma. I'm so proud of you." Harmony was nuzzling her newborn while he was still trying his best to get his legs under him.

"Will the baby ever stand, Grammy?" Annie asked.

"He will. It takes a while before those spindly little legs have enough strength to hold his body up," Lucy told her as she toweled her arm dry. She made sure the foal's navel and the bit of cord that was still attached to it were treated to prevent any infection and then she cleaned the placenta out of the stall.

Lucy came out of the stall and put her arms around Cal's waist. "Thank you again, for giving Harmony to me. I absolutely love her...and you, Cowboy." She raised her face to him and he kissed her intensely to the chagrin of the boys and the giggles of the girls.

"Come on, let's sample some of those cookies. Harmony and her baby will be all right and they need some time to bond anyway. I'll check on them in a little while," Cal said.

When they got inside, Annie immediately retrieved the letter she brought with her that morning and gave it to Cal. "This is yours, Grandpa. It came to our house. Somebody doesn't know where you live, I guess."

Cal took it and read the return address. "Tess. Well, this is a shock. She probably doesn't know where I live." He opened it, read it and chuckled. "Strange, really strange."

Lucy tilted her head in a questioning way. "Are you okay, Cal?"

"Yeah, I'm okay; perplexed, but okay. Tess hasn't contacted me or returned any messages in more than twenty years and now she sends a note with about six lines. As you like to say, Lucy, something's going on, but I don't know what. I guess we'll wait and see."

He handed the short note to Lucy. She read it and shrugged her shoulders. "Maybe you should write back so she knows you received it."

They continued to make trips to the stables to check on the baby.

When Sean arrived to pick up Amy and Doug, all four of the children interrupted each other in their efforts to tell him about Harmony and the foal. He went to the stall to see them.

"Quite a lesson in reproduction today, huh?" he asked Lucy.

She laughed. "Yep, we supply all sorts of education here at Frasier Ranch. I'll let you and Samantha fill in the details of the *beginning* of the birth process."

"Thanks. I suppose the questions were inevitable anyway and now we have a foundation to build on. I might call Samantha on the way home so she can be prepared."

"I suppose I should warn Paul and Lynne, too," Lucy said to no one in particular.

* * *

When Lucy came to bed, Cal held the covers back and waited for her to climb into bed and into his arms. "This has been an eventful day, Lucy Mae. Healthy new foal, a letter from Tess and lots of cookies," he added.

"Your grandchildren will always know the way to your heart, Cal...cookies."

"Actually, you are the way to my heart, Lucy. I had all kinds of thoughts going through my head while watching you with Harmony. I asked you to marry me and leave so much of your world behind. Instead of wearing designer clothes, you're sitting in a pile of straw in a stable. You are an amazing woman and I love you more than I can ever tell you. I would give up anything in this world as long as I had you."

She held his face in her hands and told him, "I would do it again in a heartbeat. I would rather be in jeans and boots and sitting in the stable than in a board room any day. Perhaps there are times I miss that life, a little. If I'm totally honest, maybe I miss the feelings of importance and power, but I have not regretted one day of marrying you and moving here, Cowboy." He pulled her close and kissed her.

*   *   *

In the morning, after she checked on Harmony and the foal and she and Cal said their morning prayers, she asked, "Have you asked Len to be your foreman on the other part of the ranch?"

"Yes, I did. You want to know what he said?" Cal was grinning at her.

"Of course, I do."

"He wanted to know if I had checked it out with you and if you agreed to him having the job. See the *power* you wield, Honey?"

"I guess I'm flattered that he cares about my opinion. Why would he ask that?"

"Honestly, I don't know. I believe he respects you and knows we are a team, so he was covering his behind in case you disagreed. Either way, his second question was concerning his age. He seemed to think he was too old for the job."

Lucy looked surprised. "How old is he? Fifty-five, maybe?"

"He's fifty-seven. I told him I was looking for the best man for the job, and that I was concerned about his years of experience and not his years on this earth. So, he accepted the offer. He will move his things from his apartment in town to the house on the ranch, probably this weekend."

"Good. Do you know if he has a family somewhere?" Lucy asked.

"Not that I know of. He's been a loner as long as I've known him. Some people enjoy being alone. I, on the other hand, enjoy being with a woman...but only one specific woman." He wrapped his arms around her and lifted her off the floor.

"I believe we established that fact last night, Cal," she laughed. Then she kissed him and said, "Now put me down. We both have things to do today."

Lucy's phone rang. The caller ID told her it was Leon. "Hello Leon. How's everyone in Colorado?"

"We are all terrific and Ginny says hello. I only have a minute but I have some exciting news to share. Clint and Janet are expecting a baby. I'll finally get to be a grandpa."

"I'm thrilled for them and for you. That's such a good feeling, isn't it?"

They talked for a few more minutes until Leon had someone barging through his office door. "I have to go, Lucy. I have a young man who hasn't learned the art of knocking on doors yet," he laughed.

"Blake," Leon scolded after he put his phone away. "You're going to break all the doors at Mountain House if you don't learn to open them slowly. Where did you acquire that deplorable habit?"

"I don't know. Probably one of the many places I lived. Sometimes, you had to be fast if you wanted to use the bathroom or get some food or anything. I'll try to remember. Did you want to see me?"

"Yes," Leon said. "I have some forms for you to fill out if you want to take your GED tests."

"Okay." Blake was looking at the photo of Lucy again. He gravitated toward her picture every time he was in Leon's office. He studied it as if he could will his memory to fill in the blanks.

"Did you say your sister lived in Texas, Mr. Henderson? What part of Texas?"

"She and her husband own a ranch near Magnolia. Have you ever been to Magnolia in your travels around the Southwest?"

Suddenly, Blake knew how he recognized her. "I think she threatened to shoot me one time when I was trespassing."

Leon laughed so hard he almost choked. "That would be my sister, Lucy, for sure. Do you want me to tell her you're here or should we keep that information confidential?"

Blake thought about the last time he saw her. She came to the jail where he was incarcerated and convinced him to give up his children. He knew it was the best thing for them, but it made him sad. "No, don't tell her. It wouldn't do anybody any good."

CHAPTER 10

"I'M GOING TO CHURCH TONIGHT to practice for Sunday morning service. Do you want to go along?" Cal asked.

"Let me call Phoebe. If she has the time, I'll meet her at her clothing shop while you practice."

Lucy asked Ben to check on Harmony and her baby while they were gone that evening. "I have another favor, Ben. If you're going to be anywhere close to the bunkhouse today, would you deliver this package to Alisha? If she isn't there when you get there, just leave it in the kitchen. I wrote her name on it."

"Sure. I'll be there this afternoon. She may already be gone for the day, but I'll leave it where she'll be sure to find it."

Lucy explained, "It's a couple of books we talked about during the week we cooked together. I saw them at a used book shop and thought she might like them."

* * *

Ben rode the ATV to a far pasture, checking fences before they turned the new bull in with the heifers. He had no desire to be chasing a love-crazed bull and his harem around for hours or days, so the fences better be *bull-tight*.

When he reached the bunkhouse, it didn't seem as though anyone was around. He entered the far door to leave the package. That's when he heard a female's voice. "Stop, please. Come on, Toby. I don't want to do this. Please stop."

Ben walked up behind Toby and grabbed him by the shirt and belt. In one swift motion, he jerked him clear off the floor and threw him onto one of the tables.

He turned his attention to Alisha. "Are you okay? Physically, I mean?" he asked.

She nodded and started to cry.

Ben looked at Toby, who was as white as a ghost. "What is the matter with you, Toby? Have you lost your ever-lovin' mind? I should fire you immediately but I want to hear some kind of explanation before I turn you loose on society to attack some other girl."

"I...I wasn't attacking her. I like Alisha, a lot, Mr. Frasier, and I thought she liked me. I would never hurt her. You have to believe me."

"Did you hear her saying 'no' and 'stop,' Toby? What do you think a girl means when she says those words?"

Toby was shaking his head. "I don't know...I was just trying to kiss her. I wasn't going to do anything else. I thought all girls said no...but didn't mean it."

Ben was looking at him like he was from another planet. "Who in the world told you that?"

"My dad. He said all kinds of things about women. I guess he was wrong, huh?"

Toby was just a kid and Ben almost felt sorry for him. Obviously, no one had ever talked to him about relationships when he was growing up or exhibited the right kind of behavior, either.

"Go outside and wait for me, Toby. We need to talk some more."

After he left, Ben turned to Alisha, who was standing in the same place as when he walked in. She had stopped crying but looked as if she might faint any minute.

"Alisha, do you want to tell me what happened here?"

She nodded and swallowed hard. "Sometimes, if Toby's done working for the day, he'll stop by here and help me clean up or we just set and talk about stuff. Nothing important, y'know? I like him and we have gone for walks and even held hands sometimes. But today...I don't know, maybe I sent the wrong message or something, but he had his arms around me so tight, I couldn't move and even if I did want him to kiss me some time, it wouldn't be like that." She started to cry again.

Ben silently asked God for some of the wisdom his father always seemed to have. "Listen to me, Alisha. You didn't do anything to deserve that kind of treatment, even if you were flirting. A real man...young or old...has to listen when a woman says no. Do you understand what I'm saying? This is not your fault and I do not want you to feel any guilt about it."

She nodded. "Okay." Then she said, so quietly Ben almost didn't hear her. "Mr. Frasier, please don't fire him. He needs this job and..." her lip quivered as she said, "I still do like him. Is that a terrible thing to say?"

"No, it isn't terrible. I understand, but there will have to be some consequences for his behavior. I'll decide after I talk to him some more. Do you want me to take you home?"

She shook her head. "No, I'll be fine. Thank you." She managed a tremulous smile.

Ben walked outside and found Toby sitting on the ground with his arms wrapped around his knees and his head down. "I really messed up, didn't I, Mr. Frasier?"

"I think that's an understatement, Toby. I'm ashamed to think one of our employees would act like that. If it's any consolation, Alisha asked me not to fire you. I'm going to give you a week off without pay, but I think we need to have some long talks about acceptable behavior. No man ever won a girl's heart by force. That isn't what being a man is all about, and I don't know what your father told you, but you need to get all of that out of your head."

Toby nodded. "I understand. I'll stay away for a week, and thank you for allowing me to keep my job. It won't ever happen again."

Ben believed him but reminded him, "It better never happen again or I will personally press charges. Then I'll fire you. One more thing, Toby. I'm not going to mention this to the other guys, but if I hear one word of you bragging about your actions, the deal is off and you will be terminated immediately."

As Ben made his way home, he wondered if God was preparing him for the trials of fatherhood when his babies got a little older or if he was being prepared to be the sole owner of the ranches. Neither thought gave him much comfort. One thing he knew for sure: his boys would be taught how to treat a woman, just as his dad had taught him.

*   *   *

After Luke was asleep, Ben and Candy sat together on the couch. He put his arm around her shoulders and pulled her to him. He told her about the incident with Toby, knowing she would not tell anyone.

"You know, Candy, when I think about being solely in charge without Dad to advise me, it scares me to death. Sometimes being a parent scares me to death, too." He placed his hand on her swollen belly. "I can't begin to tell you how much I love you and Luke and these babies we haven't seen yet. I pray every day I will be a good husband and father."

"Ben, you *are* a good husband and father. You are truly a good man, Honey. I could never ask for a better partner to spend my life with. It sounds as though you handled the situation today with all the wisdom your father would have. I'm proud of you and I love you so much." She kissed him and held him close.

* * *

Lucy lay on the couch with her head on Cal's lap. "So, tell me how practice went tonight."

Cal ran his fingers through her hair. "It was good, I think. At least, I didn't get fired before Sunday morning. We practiced a few songs that I will have to work on here at home. They were new to me, but most of the others were familiar. How was Phoebe's clothing shop?"

"Whew, she has her work cut out for her right now. Once she gets some more shelving and clothes racks, it will be much more organized. At the moment, it looks like a hurricane swept through. We made some progress tonight and I think she has another volunteer helping tomorrow. Her heart is in this and in helping victims of domestic violence, so she will get it done or die trying. She's a determined woman."

"That sounds like someone else I know," Cal laughed. "It's no wonder you two have been friends for so long."

"Have you decided if you're going to answer your sister's letter?"

"I'm struggling with that. I guess I'm holding a grudge, aren't I? Will you help me write it so I don't become too sarcastic?"

"Yes, I will, but I think we should invite her to come and stay for a week. You two really do need to become reacquainted. Remember when you told me life was too short to continue to hate Leon?"

"You're going to use my own words against me, aren't you?" he chuckled. "Okay, we'll invite her but I think I'm safe because I will bet you she won't accept the invitation."

"You're on. I accept the bet. Wait…what are we wagering?"

Cal smiled down at her. "I'm sure we'll think of something, Lucy."

CHAPTER 11

CANDY WAS EXCITED about the imminent arrival of her parents. She was hoping their news was that they were going to be re-married. Ben struggled within himself whether or not to tell her why they were really coming.

"You know, Honey, I don't want you to have your hopes dashed if they aren't going to be remarried. They've been apart for a lot of years," he cautioned her.

Candy nodded her understanding. "I know, but I also know they've been talking almost every day so that's a good sign they must be able to tolerate each other," she laughed.

* * *

Lucy helped Cal draft a letter to Tess. He gave an abbreviated version of their life; number of grandchildren, the combining of the two ranches and of course, the new address. He invited her to come for a week in July to help him celebrate his birthday. He assured her she could stay in the guest house and have her privacy. It was short and to the point.

* * *

Everyone was present in church on Sunday. Samantha and Sean and the kids drove from Houston and Jackie and Gary came from Beaumont. With Phoebe and Jerry, too, that was twenty-one people plus the three babies. They all laughingly agreed Cal had his own fan club. Although Lucy was proud of him and loved watching him with the praise team, she also missed worshiping with him beside her. Gabe was watching Cal intensely. Gary hung on to him or he might have joined Cal up front.

When the pastor asked for prayer requests, Devon stood and said, "I need a new kidney if anyone has a spare." Vicki nearly died of embarrassment, but everyone else thought he did what he needed to do.

Reservations had been made at a local restaurant, so the noisy crowd gathered there after church. Cal told everyone he would probably need to fill in for the other guitar player for a few more Sundays and while he was thoroughly enjoying the experience, he would be happy to be back with his family to worship. During the meal, Paul jokingly told Lucy, "Mom, you are in so much trouble for the education you and Harmony provided when the kids were there."

"I've been in trouble before," she told him. Then she added, "Actually, I thought I was doing you a favor by providing the visuals." Everyone found that quite humorous.

Samantha asked if she was going to come teach the rest of the course now that they had the visuals in their heads. "Nope. That's your job. Sorry," was Lucy's reply.

* * *

Before they left for home, Lucy asked Jackie if she and Gary would like to have a weekend away. She and Cal would watch Gabe and Michael at their house or at the ranch; wherever they thought the boys would be more comfortable. Jackie promised to consider the offer and let them know.

Ben asked Lucy if she would pick Myrna and Frank up at the airport when they arrived because he didn't think he could remain civil on their ride home. She agreed to do as he asked.

* * *

"Well, look who came to pick us up, Myrna," Frank said as he spotted Lucy waiting by the baggage claim area. He gave her a hug and Myrna did, also. They looked happy, Lucy thought, but she still had reservations about this visit.

"Can we both stay in the guest house, Lucy?" Myrna asked.

"Cal and I discussed that, Myrna, but we really prefer you stay in separate rooms since you aren't married. That may seem old-fashioned but it is a rule at our house. I'm sure you understand."

"We do understand and we do plan on getting married again. In fact, that's why we came now. We want to ask Candy's blessing and have her and Ben be our witnesses when we go to the courthouse to be married."

Lucy nearly drove off the side of the road. Maybe they didn't plan on telling Candy about her birth and Frank's unfaithfulness.

Frank continued, "But first, we need to confess the past to Candy and ask for her forgiveness."

'Oh, damn,' Lucy said to herself. 'I thought maybe we dodged the bullet, but I guess not.'

"You know, Candy is due to have those babies in the next month. Aren't you afraid she will be so upset about your confession, it might throw her into early labor?" Lucy asked.

"Candy is tough. I think she will be okay," Frank said. "We could have waited until after the babies were born, but we want to be married as soon as possible."

"While I understand wanting to be married, it seems pretty selfish to me," Lucy told them. "You aren't thinking about your daughter's feelings at all."

Myrna considered what she said. "Maybe you're right...but we're here now. We may as well go ahead with our original plans."

Frank took Myrna's bags to the guest house, then took his luggage to the upstairs bedroom, located over the great room.

*   *   *

Ben told Candy, "Your parents are here and getting settled in. Would you like me to ask them to come here to our house or do you want to sit in the great room to talk? Or we could go out to the patio. Where would you be more comfortable?"

Candy laughed. "You're kidding, right? I'm not comfortable anywhere. I guess our house would be the best. I can't wait to see them and hear what the surprise is."

Ben looked at her and wanted so badly to warn her of the storm that was coming her way. Instead, he said, "I love you, Candy and I'll be here for you. Don't forget that, okay?"

He took Luke to Lucy and asked her to watch him for the next few hours.

*   *   *

As soon as Frank and Myrna were unpacked, they went to Ben and Candy's house.

"Where's that sweet baby boy?" Frank asked.

"He's at Dad's right now," Ben said. "I'll go get him when we're done talking."

"Well, Candy, as you know, your mother and I have been talking nearly every day since we were here when Luke was born." He held Myrna's hand and smiled at her. "We've discussed so many things and finally decided our phone bills would be more affordable if we lived closer to each other. Like, maybe in the same house."

So, are you telling me you are going to be remarried?" Candy asked.

"Yes, we want to be, but we have some things to discuss with you first."

Candy shook her head. "You're adults; you don't need my permission to get married."

Myrna looked at Frank and said, "It isn't your permission we're asking for, Candy. It's your forgiveness."

Candy had an uncomfortable look on her face as she asked, "Forgiveness for what?"

'There is no easy way to tell this story, Candy, so I will start at the beginning. After your mother and I had the four boys, we were so busy with all the things that constitute family activities and my long work hours, we grew apart. There was nothing between us anymore. I found a young woman who made me feel important and attractive and needed. We had an affair." He took a deep breath. "We obviously weren't careful and she became pregnant. I wasn't the kind of man who would abandon her in that situation so I stayed. I was going to ask your mother for a divorce after the baby was born but things didn't work out that way. When she had the baby, there were complications," Frank paused and took a deep breath, "and she died."

Candy had not said a word, but now she asked, "So what happened to the baby?"

Ben closed his eyes and tightened his grip on her shoulders, waiting for the rest of the story.

"That baby girl was you, Candy," Frank said. "I couldn't abandon you or place you for adoption, so I asked your mother to forgive me and allow me to bring you into our family. I was never unfaithful again, but she never really, in her heart, forgave me, either."

Ben fully expected Candy to cry or scream at them or something, but he was unprepared for her response. Quietly, she said, "So, let me get this straight...you had an affair and were prepared to divorce your wife but when your girlfriend died, you found it inconvenient to raise a child by yourself so you crawled back home. Then you allowed your wife and sons to treat that little girl like a piece of dirt her whole life. Now you've decided you love each other again and want my forgiveness and blessing so you can get remarried. Is that about the entire story?"

Before either of them could answer, Candy stood and said, "I won't give you my forgiveness or my blessing. You can do whatever you want, but I don't ever want to see either of you again as long as I live. Do you understand me? You are both dead to me. You will never see Luke or these new babies, either. I'm done with this conversation."

She held her hand out to Ben and he went outside with her. They walked in silence for a while. Then she turned to him and started to cry and couldn't stop. He held her as tightly as he could and allowed her to cry as long as she needed to. She slumped down onto a glider on the patio. Ben sat beside her. "I'm so sorry, Candy," was all he could say.

They sat there for what seemed like hours. He could only imagine the thoughts that were going through her mind. "Do you want me to ask Dad and Lucy to keep Luke for the night?"

She nodded and waited while he left to ask them. When he returned, they went inside and curled up on the bed. Ben stayed as close to her as possible and wiped her tears every time a new wave of sadness came over her. He had never felt so totally helpless about a situation in his entire life.

*   *   *

Ben went to get Luke in the morning. "Did Candy sleep at all last night?" Cal asked him.

He shook his head. "She won't get out of bed this morning. She won't eat or drink anything, not even a cup of tea or a piece of toast. She hasn't even asked about Luke. I'm very worried." He looked imploringly at Lucy. "Do you think you could come over and talk to her for a little bit?"

Lucy told him she would be there in a few minutes. She and Cal prayed together that she would have the right words to comfort Candy. Ben was feeding Luke when she got there. He motioned for her to go to the bedroom. Candy was lying on her side with her legs pulled up as far as her belly would allow. She looked as though she was asleep, but when Lucy pulled a chair to the side of the bed, she opened her eyes.

"Candy, Honey, I am so sorry for what you're going through." Lucy pushed her pretty red curls off her face and stroked her head. "I want to tell you how much Cal and I love you and I'm here to listen or talk or cry with you. You are a very special person and you can't let someone else's mistakes define who you are."

Candy reached for her hand and squeezed it. "I want to go to sleep and never wake up," she said so softly Lucy could barely hear her.

"I know, Sweetheart, but Ben and Luke need you and these new babies need you, too."

"I should never have gotten married nor had children. What if I treat them like I was treated? Abuse continues generation after generation, I know."

Lucy couldn't bear to see her like this. "Candy, listen to me. You are a wonderful wife and mother. You will never be emotionally abusive to your children. God has given you a mother's heart, tender and nurturing, and God never makes mistakes."

Candy smiled for a second, then she closed her eyes and shook her head as if she didn't believe it.

"Candy, maybe this information, as damaging as it was, is in reality a blessing in disguise. You spent your entire life thinking you were unloved by your mother because of some fault of yours. Now you know it had nothing to do with you. Myrna was angry at your father, not you. There was nothing you could have done to prevent it."

Candy seemed to digest that information and grasp what Lucy was telling her. Her face was flushed and she grimaced even when she had her eyes closed. Lucy felt her forehead again. She definitely had a fever. When Lucy pulled the covers back a bit, she wasn't surprised to see Candy's clothes were wet.

She went to Ben. "You need to get Candy to the hospital as soon as possible. I believe her water has broken and she's beginning to have contractions. Leave Luke with me. Cal will drive you. Stay next to her and keep her talking or at least opening her eyes every little bit. I'll call her doctor and tell him you're on the way."

"She's not due for another two weeks. Are you sure she's in labor? Is it the stress of last night?"

"Twins often come early, Ben, but she seems to be in shock to me. Her skin is clammy and she has a temperature. She is severely depressed. If she goes into full-blown shock, you could lose her. Now go."

Lucy grabbed Luke and went to her house. "Cal?" she called. "You need to drive Ben and Candy to the hospital. I'll call the doctor. She's in labor and in shock, I believe. Please be safe but hurry." She gave him a quick kiss as he went out the door.

Ben picked Candy up and carried her to the car. He got in and seat belted them in together. *'Please, God, please stay with her. I can't lose Candy. She's my life,'* he prayed.

"Candy, Sweetheart, open your eyes and talk to me." He continued to talk to her all the way to the hospital. She occasionally opened her eyes and said a word or two. When Cal pulled into the emergency room entrance, they were met by medical staff with a gurney. They placed Candy on it and whisked her inside and down the hall. Ben followed as far as he could but then had to wait to put on a gown and mask.

Cal parked the car and returned to the waiting room. He wished Lucy had come with him, but time was of the essence and there wasn't time to put Luke in a car seat. He called the other children to let them know what was going on and told them their prayers would be appreciated.

CHAPTER 12

"SO, TELL ME, TESS...did you ever send the note to your brother like we discussed?" Sandi asked.

"Yes, believe it or not, I did finally send it and wonder of wonders, he wrote back."

Sandi laughed. "See, that wasn't so hard, was it?"

Tess shook her head. "Harder than you will ever know, Sandi. I had to force myself to do it."

"Sometimes forcing ourselves is the only way to accomplish anything. You know, the clichés about getting out of your comfort zone and all that."

"Well, let me tell you about getting out of my comfort zone. He asked me to come stay at the ranch for a week so we could become reacquainted. He even said I could stay in the guest house so I would have my privacy."

"Tess, that sounds wonderful. That's exactly what you should do. You're not working so you don't have to take vacation days."

"Sandi, did you forget I said I hate Texas? Why would I want to spend a week there?"

"Tess, you don't know if you hate Texas or not. You only know your mother said *she* hated Texas. Am I right?"

Tess nodded. "Yes, you're right, but I still don't know if I could go there or not. What would I say to him? 'Oh, I'm sorry I haven't talked to you or acknowledged any of your invitations or celebrations in the last twenty years, but, gee, I'd really like to be pals now.'"

Sandi told her, "Think of it like this, Tess. Wouldn't it be better to establish a bit of a friendship now before you may really need to ask him if you can live there permanently?"

"I won't ever have to ask that. I have sent more resumes and applied to several places online. I'm sure someone will call."

"The clock is ticking, Tess. Have you talked to the management at your apartment complex about downgrading to a less expensive apartment? Have you sold any of your treasures?"

"No to both of those questions. But I have someone interested in one of the paintings. If I can sell that, I could pay another month's rent."

Sandi changed tactics as she was making no headway. "Tell me how you feel about this situation you find yourself in."

"I feel like a failure. I have some monster headaches which I attribute to constantly being concerned about the next bill I have to pay."

"Have you seen a doctor about the headaches? You still have insurance for another month or two, correct?"

"Yes, but I can't afford the co-pay. It's a vicious cycle. The headaches come from worrying about the bills and I can't get help for them because it would be another bill."

Sandi glanced at Tess' purse. "Is that a new bag, Tess?"

"Oh, I knew you would notice that. Yes, I thought I deserved a small reward for sending out the resumes."

"You have a shopping addiction, Tess. It doesn't matter if you have the money or not, you spend it anyway."

"I know. I always have loved to shop. My mother loved to shop."

"Your assignment for your next visit is to keep a journal of every cent you spend. Food, clothing, bills, everything; no matter how small. I'm not going to scold you, so keep it honest. We'll discuss it when you come back."

"One more thing, Tess. Seriously consider taking your brother up on his offer."

* * *

Lucy knocked on the door of the guest house. Frank and Myrna were watching television. "He's going back to his place when this program is over," Myrna said. She seemed to think Lucy was coming to complain about the two of them being together.

Lucy waved it aside. "I didn't come to see where you were. I came to tell you Candy is at the hospital. She seems to be in shock and I believe the twins are arriving earlier than expected."

"Oh no," Myrna said. "Is that because of what we told her last night?"

"I would certainly think that had something to do with it, although it may not be the sole cause of it."

"Should we go to the hospital or do you think that would do more harm than good?" Frank asked.

"You have to make that decision. Cal is with them now. My suggestion would be to stay here and talk to God about it. There isn't anything you can do there. I just wanted you to be aware of what was happening."

Frank walked to where Lucy was standing. He stroked Luke's head. "He is a beautiful little boy. It breaks my heart to know we will probably never get to know him and he won't know us." With tears in his eyes, he looked at Myrna. "Not being able to watch Luke grow up is the consequence of my actions so long ago. I will never forgive myself for that."

Lucy couldn't think of any comforting words to say at the moment.

She carried Luke back to her house. "My sweet boy, Luke. Your mommy has to be okay, doesn't she? You and your daddy would be so lost without her."

* * *

"Has your dad called again, Jackie?" Gary asked. "It seems like they should know something by now."

"No, not yet. Maybe Candy wasn't in labor. Maybe it was a false alarm."

"I guess that's possible. Have you thought any more about the offer Lucy and your dad made to stay with the boys while we get away for a weekend?"

"Not really. Have you? Do you have some place in mind?" she asked him.

"There's a nice hotel not too far away where we could swim and golf and just relax. Or we could go to one of the state parks and rent a cabin and run around naked in the woods," he said with a serious expression.

Jackie laughed. "With my luck, I'd fall in a patch of poison ivy. I think I'll vote for the hotel."

"The next question is should they stay here with the boys or should the boys stay with them at their house?"

"I was thinking about that. Let's take the boys there. That way the contractors can work on the remodeling while no one is here. They won't have any interruptions and Gabe won't be upset by all the noise of saws and hammering."

"Yeah, I guess. I really hope we made the right decision when we suggested Dad should come to live with us. His health has been going downhill ever since Mom died several years ago, but I don't want him to go to a nursing home and he really can't live by himself anymore."

"I know, Honey," Jackie told him. "You are doing the right thing for your dad."

She hoped it was the right thing for their family, too. Would they be able to handle the alterations to their lives? Especially Gabe, who didn't like changes to his routine? She didn't know the answers, but she knew Gary felt a need to take care of his father, and she would support him in that decision as long as she could.

*   *   *

Ben came out to talk to Cal. He sat down and put his head in his hands and cried.

Cal put his hand on his back. "Tell me, Ben. What's going on?"

Ben lifted his head. "Well, we have a little boy and a little girl. They're both slightly underweight, of course, and they're in the neo-natal unit. But Candy is in ICU. She's not doing well, Dad."

Cal put his arms around Ben like he used to do when he was a little boy and cried about something. "It will be okay, Son. She's a strong woman and God knows these babies need her. And you and Luke do, too."

"It's my fault. I should never have let Frank and Myrna come. I knew about it and still I allowed them to destroy her world. What kind of husband am I?"

"You can't blame yourself, Ben. We don't know for sure this wouldn't have happened anyway. Twins are often born early. No matter how angry you are at Candy's parents, you know they would never have *wanted* this to happen."

"I'm going back to be with Candy and the babies. No one else is allowed to be in the room so I'll rotate between them. I'm not coming home until we all come home, Dad." He turned and went through the doors. Cal called Lucy.

*   *   *

Ben sat by Candy's bedside and talked to her, although he got no response. "Candy...Honey, we got that little girl you wanted to name Sophia, and a beautiful little boy, too. Samuel...remember, you said you wanted to name a boy, Samuel? Please open your eyes, Sweetheart. I need you to look at me." He put his head down on the bed. *'Please, heavenly Father, let her live. I love her so.'* He closed his eyes for what he thought was a few minutes, but he fell asleep from exhaustion. He heard a whispered, "Ben?"

"Candy, I'm right here." He stood and bent over to kiss her forehead.

"What happened, Ben? The last thing I remember was Lucy talking to me."

"I know. She told me to get you to the hospital quickly because you were in shock. I thought I was going to lose you, Candy."

She still looked confused and disoriented. "Where are the babies? Are they okay? I want to see them." She threw the covers off and started to swing her legs over the side of the bed.

"Whoa. You can't get out of bed, Candy. I'll get a nurse. You just woke up. You're not going anywhere. They're taking good care of our babies, I promise."

She lay back down and closed her eyes again. "Ben? I love you."

When the nurse came to check on Candy, Ben left to tell Cal she was awake.

"She woke up for a little bit, Dad. Then she closed her eyes again, but I think she is going to be all right."

Cal hugged him and sent him back to her. Then he called Lucy.

"Lucy? Candy opened her eyes and spoke a few words to Ben. I'll be home as soon as I can. Call the kids and tell them, please. I'm so grateful, Lucy. I was truly worried. I know she's not out of the woods yet, but at least she said some words."

CHAPTER 13

LEON SPENT SEVERAL HOURS on routine paperwork. Then he reluctantly filled out the forms for Bruce Halloway to be transferred back to the court system, which ultimately meant he would go to prison. He simply could not remain at Mountain House any longer. His presence there was a disruptive and destructive force.

He refused to cooperate in any way, about anything. He was continually involved in altercations with the other residents. While they undoubtedly were at fault occasionally, Bruce was almost always the instigator. Although Leon had tried to convince him it would be in his best interest to make some constructive changes in his life and behaviors, he adamantly refused to consider the alternatives.

Bruce rarely, if ever, took responsibility for his actions. Leon leaned back in his desk chair and considered how many years of his own life had been spent refusing to take responsibility for his actions or the consequences of those actions. He had lived in denial for many years. If he hadn't been found on a street and sent to Mountain House, he undoubtedly would have died. God rescued him for a reason. He firmly believed it was to help other young men who found themselves in that same situation.

It saddened him when that wasn't possible, but he always believed they might need someone else's guidance and drew comfort from thinking he was sending them to the next helper God had in mind.

Leon walked down the hall to his son's office. It never failed to make him smile when he saw the plaque on the door that read, 'Pastor Clint Henderson.' He was truly blessed and he knew it.

"Clint?" he said as he entered. "I would like to ask Bruce to come to your office where I can tell him he's going to be transferred back to the court system. That way, there will be two of us. You can serve as the witness. I've made arrangements for the police officer to pick him up. He should be here in a few minutes. I didn't want to give Bruce advance warning for fear he'd run. The officer can escort him to gather his things."

"I know this bothers you, Leon, but you have done everything possible to make his stay here beneficial for him and he has chosen to be uncooperative. He's a man, not a teenager, and he's making his own choices, no matter how bad those choices are."

Leon nodded. He asked one of the residents to have Bruce come to Clint's office. In the meantime, the officer arrived. When Bruce entered, he was his usual surly, defiant self.

"Bruce, I'm sorry to tell you that Officer Taylor is here to escort you back to the jail where you were before you came to Mountain House. This has not been a beneficial experience for you, but perhaps your next stop will be."

Bruce narrowed his eyes and stood. The string of expletives that rolled off his tongue was extensive. "The next stop? The next stop?" he shouted. "We both know what the next stop is, and I doubt it will be beneficial."

With that, he whirled around and grabbed Officer Taylor's gun from his holster. He stood with his back to the door while he motioned for the three of them to stay across the room from him. "I am not going to prison. Do you hear me, all you sanctimonious bastards? I am not going back. I'm sure now that I have the upper hand in this room, we can come to some sort of agreement. Don't you think so, *Pastor*?" he said with a loathing that was unmistakable.

"Well, now, let's see. I'm going to need some money. You...," he pointed the gun at Leon, "...have someone bring any money that you keep here. Then I want a car brought around to the back door."

Leon took a step toward him. Bruce warned him, "Don't move."

"Okay, Bruce. I won't move, but listen for a minute. There is no money kept at Mountain House. We don't have a safe or anything like that. There is nowhere anyone here can get money for you."

"That's too bad." He seemed to think about an alternative plan. "Okay, all of you...empty your wallets."

They did as they were told and handed him the bills. He took them and shoved them in his pocket. "It might get me a tank of gas, at least."

At that moment, the door was pushed open with such force, it slammed into Bruce and knocked him off balance. He fell into the desk and lost his grip on the gun. Clint scrambled for it and held it while the officer was busily attempting to place handcuffs on Bruce.

"I'm sorry for opening the door so hard again, Mr. Henderson," Blake Tanner apologized, before he realized the scene that had just played out in front of him.

Leon laughed and told him, "Right now, Blake, I could hug you for that bad habit."

* * *

When all the excitement was over and Bruce had been taken away, Leon sat in Clint's office and shook his head. "Well, we never know what a day will bring when we leave home in the morning, do we?"

Clint replied, "That's a true statement. Wow, I own some guns but I don't know if anyone has ever held a gun on me before."

"I'm sure it happened to me many times when I was on the streets or cheating at poker tables, but the fortunate thing is I don't remember much of that life," Leon said.

"Are you planning on telling Ginny?" Clint asked him.

"Yes, I will. We keep no secrets from each other. Besides, this will probably make the evening television report, especially if it's a slow news day. I truly wish Bruce had not added to his charges. It will be worse for him now."

* * *

Lucy took Luke to Lynne the next day, so she could go to the hospital. She and Cal packed some clean clothes and a few personal items to take with them for Ben. They weren't allowed in Candy's room, but they went with Ben to see the twins. They looked so tiny but healthy. Lucy hugged Ben. "Congratulations on two more beautiful children."

* * *

Frank and Myrna asked to speak to Cal and Lucy before they left. It was an awkward situation and no one knew where to start. Finally, Myrna said, "Candy has every right to hate me. I will admit I emotionally abused her for many years. She was a constant reminder of what her mother must have looked like with her red hair, turned up nose and freckles. I believe I was trying my best to punish Frank and instead, I ruined a little girl's life. And I almost caused her to lose her life because of my selfish need to confess that to her. I will never be able to forgive myself for that. I don't expect her to ever want to see me, but I pray she will talk to Frank again. He always took good care of her and tried to be a loving father to her. That made me angry and jealous, too. After we were here for Luke's birth, I began to see a counselor. I knew I should have done that when Candy was a baby, but unfortunately, I didn't. Frank and I went to counseling together after we found out we still loved each other after all these years. We've discussed it and have decided to get married when we get back, but if Candy will agree to see him, Frank can come by himself."

Even though she knew Myrna had been horrible to Candy, Lucy's heart was hurting for her. At least she recognized what she had done and was taking responsibility for it. They drove them to the airport and then went to the hospital to tell Ben what had been said. He made no comment and Lucy knew it would take time for him to come to terms with the whole situation.

* * *

It was several days before Candy was moved out of ICU. Jackie, Samantha, Vicki and Lynne made good use of the time by coming to arrange the bedroom where the twins were going to sleep when they came home. It wasn't quite ready when Candy made her unexpected trip to the hospital. They spent most of the day putting baby clothes away and trying to arrange everything for the easiest possible access for Candy and Ben.

When they took a lunch break, Lucy asked Lynne what she thought of the idea of allowing Annie to come in the afternoons and help Candy with Luke. "She could certainly play with him and read to him. That would allow Candy to nap if the babies sleep at the same time, which they probably won't," she laughed.

Lynne thought it was a great idea and suggested it could even be a part of Annie's school work. She agreed to ask Paul.

* * *

Ben divided his time between the hospital and home. He couldn't abandon Luke for days at a time. Even though they had tried to prepare him for the twins' birth, suddenly having two babies in his little domain was going to be enough of a shock to Luke without wondering why his mommy and daddy disappeared, too. Ben read stories to Luke and took him riding, which of course, was Luke's favorite activity. On a rainy day or before bedtime, they would play with Legos. Luke's idea of finding the ones he wanted was to dump the entire bucket in the middle of the floor.

"It's time for a bath and then you need to get ready for bed, Luke," Ben told him.

"Nooo, Daddy. Build one more tower?" Luke pleaded.

Ben smiled at his little architect. "Okay. One more very short tower. Then we have to pick up all these pieces, okay?"

Luke was happy to help. They practiced the names of colors as they placed each brightly-colored piece into the bucket.

Bedtime was a ritual in itself. A bath, brushing teeth, prayers and lots of hugs and kisses preceded being officially tucked in. Ben enjoyed it as much as Luke did. When he knew Luke was sound asleep, Ben grabbed a bottle of water from the kitchen and made his way through the dark living room on the way to the front porch.

"Ouch! Darn! What was that?!?" Ben was yelling as he hopped around on one foot while trying not to fall over completely. He sat on the floor and found the offending Lego he had just stepped on.

Luke came wandering out of his bedroom, rubbing his eyes. "Whatcha doin', Daddy?"

"I think we missed one, Buddy," Ben told him as he held the Lego up for Luke to see. "Daddy stepped on it and it hurt. Sorry I woke you."

"Red," Luke told him.

Ben laughed, even though his ankle was killing him. "Yep. You're right, Luke. It definitely is a red one. Why don't you climb back into bed? I'm going to get some ice for my ouchie." He hopped to the kitchen and filled a bag with ice, then proceeded to the couch so he could raise his throbbing ankle.

That's where he found himself in the morning; on the couch with a bag of water now that the ice had melted, and an ankle that was purple and swollen. He really needed to go to the hospital to be with Candy, but perhaps he could see the doctor on his way there. He called Lucy and asked for help.

"And just exactly how do you plan on driving anywhere, Ben?" Lucy asked when she saw his ankle.

"I will take care of Luke. Your dad or Len can take you to the doctor's office and I'll ask Lynne to go sit with Candy until you can get there, okay?"

*   *   *

Arrangements were made and by the time Ben showed up in Candy's room, he had a walking cast on one foot. "The x-rays showed there's nothing broken. It's a bad sprain and I can lose the cast in a few days, probably. But I will have to keep it wrapped and not put any undue weight or strain on it, which makes me pretty useless for most situations."

Candy nodded in agreement and thought she would like the fact that Ben could stay with her.

It was over a week before Candy and the twins were released from the hospital. Luke was so excited to see Candy, he cried. He wasn't so sure about the babies.

* * *

Lucy called Leon and Ginny to let them know everyone was back home and doing well.

Ginny told her, "It sounds like you've had some excitement at your house. I'm so happy it has turned out positively for everyone. Please tell Ben and Candy we are keeping all of them in our prayers. Now, I'm going to give the phone to Leon and he can tell you about his exciting day."

Leon started at the beginning, not leaving out any details. When he got to the last part, he said, "We have a resident who continually comes into rooms like a bulldozer and I always chastise him for it, but today, when Blake Tanner came busting through that door, I could have kissed him."

There was silence on the other end of the phone. "Lucy? Did I lose you? Are you still there?"

Finally, Lucy found her voice and asked, "Leon, did you say Blake Tanner?"

"Yes, I did. He actually recognized your picture in my office. He said you threatened to shoot him for trespassing once upon a time."

"Leon, he is the father of the children Victoria and David adopted. I've been searching for him for weeks. Devon needs a kidney transplant and Blake may be his only hope of having a biological matching donor. I cannot believe he's at Mountain House. Don't let him out of your sight until I can tell David and Vicki about this, okay?"

"He's not going anywhere, Lucy. But aren't you assuming a lot? What if he doesn't want to be a donor?"

"I know that's a possibility, Leon, but if David and Vicki agree, I would like to come talk to him about it. No pressure; and I assure you I won't threaten to shoot him."

Leon laughed at her, "Okay, no pressure. If you come, make sure you bring Cal with you this time, okay?"

When she finished talking to Leon, Lucy sat on Cal's lap and wrapped her arms around his neck. "Get your boots on, Cowboy. We'll go tell Vicki and David the good news and then let's go to the tavern in Cypress and do some line dancing and eat wings and drink beer."

Cal laughed at her. "Really? That's what you want to do tonight? You don't even like beer. And I may need more than one to persuade me to get up and line dance."

"Okay. You drink a beer or two, we'll both dance and I'll be the one to drive home. How does that sound?

She pulled him to his feet. "I think we've put in some pretty long days lately and we need a diversion. Let's do something fun that has nothing to do with the ranch or our children or grandchildren or hospitals or people and their problems."

Cal stood and said, "Okay, Baby, if that's where you want to go...let's go."

They had a wonderful time and thoroughly enjoyed the evening. When they came home, and were standing outside on the porch, Cal had his arms around her and was nuzzling her neck. He was singing a song to her that the fiddle player had everyone singing at the bar.

'Rock me, mama, like a wagon wheel'....he continued to sing the entire chorus.

Lucy listened, enjoying the sound of his voice. With her arms around his neck, she smiled and told him, "Keep singin', Cowboy, because this mama is gonna rock your world tonight."

CHAPTER 14

CAL TOLD LUCY AFTER CHURCH on Sunday, "Ken, the leader of the praise team, asked me if I would go with the group to a church in San Antonio. It seems they've been asked to provide the music for a weekend retreat and the person I replaced is unable to travel yet. You can come along and we could stay for a few extra days. How does that sound? The River Walk, the Alamo, lots of fun things to see and do," he coaxed.

"I would love to go, Cal, but I think I should stay close for a while. Candy and Ben have their hands full and Candy is obviously not back to her former self yet. If you add Ben's recently injured ankle to the mix, I want to be available if they need me."

"Then maybe I won't go either," Cal told her.

"Of course you're going to go, Cal. They need you and it isn't like you'll be gone for a week; it's just a weekend, correct?"

He nodded. "Yes, but it would be much more fun if you went too."

That made her smile. "I'm so glad you will miss me, Honey. I'll miss you, too and…oh no… I'll have to make my own coffee in the morning."

"I see," Cal teased. "That's what I'm good for; making coffee, right?"

"Believe me, you're good at a lot more things than making coffee, but you've spoiled me by having it ready every morning. I'm sure I can remember how to make it."

"I'll tell Ken I'll go. He's having a meeting before practice this evening; I'm not sure what it's about but it is mandatory, so I guess I'll be there."

*   *   *

When the adult members of the team stopped talking and Ken had their attention, he began the meeting with a prayer. Then he said, "I think it's unfortunate that we even have to discuss this issue, but the times, they are *a-changin'* as they say and I need to reiterate a few things before we go to the retreat."

"The people attending come from all walks of life, which is good because the weekend is designed to reach as many people with the gospel of Jesus Christ as possible. However, not everyone is there for the same reason. You may have individuals who desperately need a shoulder to cry on, a listening ear, or even a hug. These retreats cause many people to become very emotional. There are trained counselors they can speak with."

"Please be aware at all times of everything you say and do. Don't misunderstand me; I'm not telling you that you can't be empathetic to someone, just remember that there are cameras on phones everywhere and with all the photo programs available, *every* and I mean, *every* photo can be altered to look like something totally different than it is. I'm telling you this because last year, a man with another group tried to comfort a college-age girl by putting his arms around her when she was crying. It cost him his marriage when it was plastered all over social media. It seems the girl had a grudge against his daughter and used this to get even for something."

*   *   *

Cal repeated Ken's words to Lucy when he came home. "It really is sad that we have to be overly cautious of even saying something nice to someone because it might be misconstrued."

Lucy agreed, "It is unfortunate but I'm glad Ken reminded everyone. There are many people, like you and me, whose first instinct when someone needs consoling, is to hug them."

She continued, "Speaking of someone who needs hugs and consoling, I'm very concerned about Candy. She's had a ton of overwhelming things hit her in the last few weeks. She looks like she's coping well on the outside, but I'm terrified of what's going on in her head and heart."

"What do you mean?" Cal questioned.

"I've been observing Candy when I'm at their house and I think she's probably dealing with some post-partum depression issues. It's a very real thing and mothers who experience difficulties surrounding the birth of their children are especially susceptible. Add the whole 'Frank and Myrna drama' to the mix and I'm afraid it's more than one person can handle without some sort of counseling."

Cal looked concerned and a bit perplexed, "I think the best thing to do would be to speak to Ben. We'll forever regret it if we don't and something happens that could have been prevented."

* * *

When Cal noticed Ben was sitting on the patio for a few minutes, he went out to join him. "How are you managing, Ben? I'm sure taking care of three children is a bit daunting, right?"

"I guess you could call it daunting, Dad. I'm thinking absolute craziness might be a better word," he laughed.

Cal gently asked, "How's Candy doing? Physically and emotionally?"

Ben looked at him with eyes that were tired, "I don't know for sure. One minute she seems like the Candy I know and love and the next minute, she's crying and can't seem to stop or tell me why. She doesn't eat, she doesn't sleep, and keeps insisting she isn't a good enough mother."

Ben glanced down at his wrapped ankle. "Even though I am not happy about my injury, it probably happened at a good time. I needed to be here to help out and now I actually *have* to be here, even if I am a bit slow at moving around."

Lucy joined them on the patio and sat in a chair by Ben. "You know, Ben, your dad and I were talking about this very thing. We think perhaps you should speak to Pastor Kelly about suggesting a counselor who deals with family issues and post-partum depression. Candy will need some help dealing with all this."

Ben looked perplexed. "Do you really think so? I suppose you're right. Her entire family is dysfunctional, and she always believed it had something to do with her."

"Do you know anything about her brothers?" Cal asked him.

"Not much. One is in the military, one hasn't seen or spoken to his parents for many years and one lives in another country. Only one of them...Steve . . . seems to live a "normal" life. He's married, lives in New Mexico, and does speak to Myrna and Frank. He sent a card and apology when he couldn't attend our wedding. I'm no psychiatrist, but my guess would be they all have relationship issues because of the way their family fell apart after Frank brought Candy home. Even if they were young, I'm sure they sensed the tension in the house, and they probably blamed her for that, too. Steve is only a few years older than Candy, so perhaps he was too little to be affected by the whole sordid mess."

"I feel so bad for Candy and for you, too, Ben. That's why we believe it's imperative to find her some help before she sinks deeper into depression," Cal told him. "Depression is a horrible thing. It fills your head with many thoughts you wouldn't have if you were thinking normally. I attended a grief counseling group for a while after your mother died so I could learn to cope with my feelings of loss."

Ben nodded in agreement. "I'll talk to Pastor and get a name of someone who can help. Until then, I'll keep praying and loving her...and changing diapers," he added.

"If you and Candy need a break, even for a few hours, to take a walk or something, come and get us. Lucy and I still know how to change diapers, right Honey?"

"Yes, I believe I remember that part," Lucy laughed.

Suddenly, Ben looked inspired. "I think I have an idea that might cheer her up for a few minutes. *If* we can get all three kids asleep at the same time. One of the little things Candy was complaining about was how awful her nails looked. She wanted to have a manicure and pedicure before the babies were born, but of course, that didn't happen. She isn't supposed to go anywhere yet...but, I'll come get you if I need you."

Later, as Lucy walked through the great room and glanced out to the patio, she stopped; then quietly went back to get Cal.

They both watched, surreptitiously, the scene before them. Candy was comfortably propped up with pillows behind her back. Ben was sitting on the patio with his injured lag stretched out in front of him, with her foot in his lap and polishing her toenails. His large hands were having some trouble holding the polish brush but they were both talking and Candy was actually smiling and looking relaxed for the moment.

Cal put his arm around Lucy's shoulders and asked, "Is that one of your "What Love Looks Like" moments?"

"Yes, oh, yes, it certainly is, Cal. Besides you making coffee for me every morning, I have several of those moments involving my grandparents that I keep in my mental memory box and now I have another one to add to it."

* * *

"I know this won't fix how you feel, Candy, but maybe it will help a little," Ben told her as he painstakingly painted her nails.

"Ben, you're so good to me. I can't explain how I feel. Right now, I'm good, but then a wave of sadness and fear hits me and it threatens to suck me under. I feel like I can't control or trust any of my thoughts or feelings; they engulf me. What happened to the old me? Where did I lose myself?"

"Listen, Honey, the 'former you' is still there. You've had to deal with so much plus the extra work of the twins. Your mind and body are rebelling so you don't have to think about it. We'll find a counselor that can help you work through these feelings, okay? I called Pastor Kelly and he gave me a name. He also suggested a group of mothers who meet at a coffee shop once a week. They have all experienced what you're going through. He knows it helps when you don't feel like you're the only one who has ever dealt with this."

Ben again glanced at his wrapped ankle and reassured her. "I'm not going to leave your side until you feel better. I wouldn't leave you, anyway, but since I'm fairly restricted due to the ankle, I really won't be leaving you alone. We have enough hands to take care of the work and Len can run both ranches if Dad is unavailable. The doctor said my ankle will be healed in a week or two since it wasn't a bad sprain; I just twisted it."

CHAPTER 15

"HAVE YOU DECIDED TO ACCEPT your brother's invitation and spend a week at the ranch in July?" Sandi asked Tess at their next appointment.

"I don't know. We seem to talk about this over and over, Sandi. Why are you so insistent I go?"

"There are several reasons, Tess. You're here because we need to work on your life choices. That includes spending, employment and relationships. I believe you want a relationship with your brother and his family more than you're willing to admit. Now that you were brave enough to initiate some correspondence, you need to pursue the next step."

"What happens if I get there and absolutely hate it...and him?"

"It's only a week, Tess," Sandi laughed. "I'm fairly certain they aren't going to lock you in a dungeon or force you to brand cattle while you're there. If you hate it, then you know you'll have to think of alternatives to your plans for when you run out of money."

"My plans are to get another job, Sandi," Tess said rather testily.

"I know that, Tess, but tell me, how's that working out for you? You've been unemployed for months now and I see no progress. You continue to live with the delusion that your fairy godmother is going to wave her wand and fix all the things in your life. It's up to you, no one else. Go to Texas and take the week to figure out what it is you want to pursue. Perhaps it's something in a totally different field, but, remember this…financially…you're running out of options."

Before Tess left Sandi's office, she asked her, "How are those headaches you were talking about the last time we met?"

Tess shrugged her shoulders, "I still have them, but like everything else, I've gotten used to them. I have a doctor's appointment tomorrow. He wants to do an MRI, so I guess that's the first step."

*   *   *

Before Cal left for the weekend, he and Lucy were enjoying conversation and their morning coffee on the front porch. "Samantha and Sean and the kids are planning to come late this morning or early afternoon to see Sophia and Samuel. They asked Ben and Candy if they were okay with that and they both agreed. I don't think they'll stay long. Amy will be lovin' on the babies and Doug will want to go for a short ride if Jarrod comes down," Lucy observed.

"Remember when I said Doug seemed frightened and uncomfortable on a horse? I think he's gone with Jarrod enough, he seems to have conquered that. In fact, he worries me a little because now he acts as though he knows a lot more than he actually does," Cal told her.

"Maybe he'll come back to the middle, not too far in either direction," Lucy said.

"I hope so. Sometimes a little knowledge combined with young boy bravado makes a dangerous combination."

"I'm sure they'll be okay. They know the rules about riding and where they can go and where they can't."

"Speaking of that, I asked Len to put the bull in with the first group of heifers. He's an ornery cuss; I really prefer no one goes in that pasture until I get back."

"Does this guy have a name?" Lucy asked.

Cal chuckled. "Yes, the name on his registration papers is Barney, but I can tell you he was called a lot of names when the guys were loading him and then unloading him. He isn't a Longhorn, but he definitely knows how to use the horns he has. Why do you want to know? Planning on having a conversation with him?"

"I hope not, but in case he gets out and comes wandering up the drive, I want to know what to call him right before I shoot him."

"Oh please don't shoot him, Lucy; he cost a lot of money but more importantly, I want his bloodlines," Cal laughed.

"Okay, Sweetheart, I'm sure Barney and I will have no contact with each other. You go and have a heart-thumping retreat weekend. It will be good for you; enjoy yourself."

Cal placed his duffel bag and guitar case in the truck. He stuck his head in Ben and Candy's house to say good-bye. Candy was nursing Samuel, while Ben was trying to coax a burp out of Sophia. Luke was playing on the floor but nearly jumped into Cal's arms when he saw him. Cal picked him up. "Hey Buddy, Grandpa has to go away for the weekend. You have to take care of the ranch for me, okay? Especially since Daddy can't walk very well or ride for a while."

"Yes, sir," Luke answered, seriously. "I love you, Grandpa."

"I love you, too, Luke." Cal looked at Ben and said, "You know, it wouldn't take much from him to convince me to stay home."

"Just go, Dad. Len is here and Lucy, too. Nothing is going to happen in two days that the two of them can't handle."

Lucy was waiting for him when he came back to the truck. "I know it's only a weekend, but I feel like I'm sending you off for a year. Be careful and I'll be waiting for you when you get back."

She tilted his hat back as he encircled her with his arms and kissed her like he was leaving for a year.

Lucy prayed as he drove away, *'God, be with the whole group and let people's hearts and lives be changed this weekend.'*

* * *

Samantha, Sean, Doug and Amy arrived a little later. Jarrod and Annie were already at the house.

"Annie, why don't you and Amy ask Aunt Candy if you can watch Luke for a little while? You girls can bring him out to the great room and play with his toys with him or read some of his books to him. That way, the grown-ups can visit and hold Samuel and Sophia and Luke won't feel left out," Lucy suggested.

Jarrod and Doug went to the stables immediately, so the girls were thrilled to have time with Luke. They had cookies and milk before he fell asleep for his afternoon nap.

* * *

Several hours later, Sean knocked on Lucy's door. "Are the boys in here with you, eating all the cookies?" he laughingly asked.

"No. I haven't seen them. I thought they probably went to see the babies when they returned."

"Hmmm, we're ready to go home but I can't find the boys. You don't suppose something happened while they were riding, do you?" Sean asked with a note of worry in his voice.

"I'm sure they've just lost track of time," Lucy reassured him. "They did have you check their cinches and saddles before they left, didn't they? The rule is someone has to check before they ride. When they didn't ask me, I assumed they asked you."

"No, I didn't see them once they headed to the stables," Sean said. "I tried the phone I gave Doug for emergencies, but it goes straight to voice mail."

"They might be out of range of a tower," Lucy told him, trying to calm his fears. "We'll wait a little longer before we form a search party." She checked the time and tried calculating how many hours it would be before darkness crept in. The boys would be frightened, cold and definitely in danger when the sun set. It was still several hours before it would even begin to get dark. Hopefully, they would come riding home soon. In the meantime, she called Paul and Lynne to let them know what was going on.

Everyone tried to act as though they weren't worried but one of the parents was looking out the window or scanning the pastures beyond the barns every few minutes. Surely the boys would have reached an area of cell phone service by now. They tried reassuring each other that *boys will be boys* and they were probably just having fun and lost track of time but as the minutes and hours ticked by, no one was believing it.

Finally, Lucy couldn't stand it any longer. She changed into her riding clothes and boots, grabbed a flashlight, her revolver and her rifle. She gave Sean a pair of gloves to wear and tossed an extra rifle to him. "You're the one who knows how to ride; let's go find those boys."

She called Len and asked him to have several of their employees meet at the bunkhouse. On her way, she stopped at the office and grabbed a long cardboard tube containing the topographical maps of the ranch, before she saddled Rigbee. She told Sean to use Cal's horse, Cutter.

*   *   *

When they got to the bunkhouse, she spread the maps on a table. They were marked with dotted lines designating each section and smaller areas defining each pasture.

Len explained to the ranch hands that they were trying to locate two young boys on horseback who should have been back several hours ago. Lucy assigned various teams of men to random areas. Stan, a recent hire, who she had never met and realized he probably didn't know she was Cal's wife, said, "I don't take orders from a woman. Where's the boss?"

Lucy didn't take the time to look up from the map she was studying. "Mr. Frasier isn't here but this is my ranch, too, so you can take orders from me or you can leave…permanently."

"You didn't hire me and you can't fire me. I'm not taking orders from you," he retorted.

Lucy walked up to him and asked, "What century are you living in? I guarantee you I have fired many men in my lifetime and I can fire you without thinking twice about it. You're taking precious time away from this search for my grandsons with your medieval ideas about women so gather your things and go home. Now."

She chose Len, Danielle and Sean to come with her. They started down the path she knew Jarrod usually took when he rode although she wasn't sure he would do the same since Doug was along. "It scares me when I realize how much braver children can be when there are two of them instead of one," she commented to her group. "Len," she asked, "you're out here many days when Jarrod rides so where do you think we should start searching? Would they find the bluffs exciting or maybe the woods? We can eliminate the pastures because they can't get into any of them with the heavy gates, right?"

"Well, I suppose if they really wanted to, they could. I mean, the gates are solid, but two smart young boys could probably figure out how to unlatch 'em and ride through."

"Great," Lucy muttered. "That wasn't too reassuring."

They followed the trail and called the boys' names, on the chance they might hear them and answer. Sean continued to try Doug's phone with no success. They searched the scrub along the riverbed and checked by the windmill. It looked as though there were some recent tracks by the water tank. That's the only place the ground was damp enough to show prints. Each group had walkie-talkies because many times, cell phone signals didn't work if they were too far away from a tower or in a dead spot. Danielle checked in with the other search groups, but no one had seen them yet.

When they reached the pasture holding the heifers and Barney, Lucy's heart sank. The gate had been opened and pulled shut again. It was evident by the sloppy way it was fastened. They skirted the outside of the fence trying to locate the herd. "Ms. Frasier, if you don't mind my askin'...what happens if that bull has the boys cornered? You know, he's not gonna take kindly to something or someone interfering with his girls."

Lucy took her rifle out of the scabbard and told him, "Then we drop him, Len. I can buy a new bull. I can't replace two boys and unfortunately, we don't own a tranquilizer gun."

"Okay," was his only reply as he nodded his head.

They found the heifers with Barney in the middle of them. At the back of the group, pressed against a fence, the boys and their horses were surrounded by the cattle milling about. They sensed something was different and Barney was not looking happy about these interlopers in his pasture. Len shook his head and put his finger to his lips to let Sean and Danielle know they needed to be quiet if possible. With all the cattle bawling, it didn't seem like it would matter, but a shout would make them even more jittery.

"How are you going to tell those boys what you want them to do?' Danielle asked.

"Fortunately, we all know a few words and phrases of sign language because of Gabe, another grandson who uses it," Lucy told her. "I hope they aren't so frightened that they've forgotten all of it."

Danielle let the other men know they had located the boys, and then the four of them devised a plan to get the boys out of harm's way. Dani would stay by the gate to open it quickly when it became necessary. Sean would try to get behind the boys and stay with them to keep them moving toward the gate while Len and Lucy would do their best to cut Barney out of the group.

When Lucy caught the boys' attention, she signed for them to be quiet and to watch Sean. She also let them know they were headed to the gate where Dani was waiting.

As soon as the gate swung open and the three of them entered his space, Barney whirled around to face them. Lucy looked at Len and nodded to his left. She and Rigbee would go right.

As she looked at the huge animal mixed in with the cattle, and the horns he was prepared to use, she prayed they would all make it safely out of the pasture.

Lucy patted Rigbee's neck and then told Barney, "Okay, Big Boy, let's see what you've got."

She and Len came at him from both directions to cut him out of the herd. As hard as they tried, he slipped back in twice, but eventually, they had him separated and by himself. He was pawing the ground and snorting, trying to decide which direction to go next. Sean pushed the boys toward the gate which Dani now had opened just far enough to allow them to slip through.

Len motioned for Lucy to follow the boys which put him in the precarious position of keeping out of Barney's way by himself. Once she was out of the pasture, Lucy knelt down with her rifle. She was prepared to make sure Len could get out without being flung around like the bull riders at the rodeo. She would drop Barney in a heartbeat if it was required.

The cowboy and the bull had reached a standoff. Neither one was moving out of the other one's sight, but Barney was pawing the ground and shaking his massive head back and forth, sending slobbers flying in all directions. He did not like these strangers in his pasture and now that this horse and rider were the only ones left, he wasn't about to let them go. Len gauged the distance between himself and the gate, which Sean was prepared to swing open for him if he headed that way. He knew he couldn't make it before Barney would rip into his horse's hindquarters with those horns.

Danielle rode on the outside of the fence, trying to draw Barney's attention to herself and her horse and away from Len. She removed her hat, waving it over her head, while whooping and hollering like a demented person. When Barney half turned to follow her movements, Len saw his chance and rode hard toward the gate. Sean jerked it open just wide enough for horse and rider to escape.

When the gate clanged shut behind him, Len and Danielle were off their horses and hugging each other. Lucy stood from her squatted position and she and Sean joined their celebratory group hug. She was extremely happy it had not been necessary to shoot Barney and even happier that the boys and the adults were all safe. "We did it," Danielle yelled.

Jarrod and Doug were still too frightened to do much celebrating. As they made their way back to the house, Sean told Doug there would be consequences for disobeying all the rules. He asked Jarrod if he had persuaded Doug to go along with him on this escapade that could have cost them their lives.

Jarrod hesitated and looked at Sean and then at Doug. Before any more could be said, Doug spoke up, "It was my idea, Dad. Jarrod said we should have someone check our saddles and stuff before we went riding and then he tried to talk me out of going into that pasture, but I told him he was a coward and we should go. It wasn't his fault at all."

Chapter 16

"WHEN ARE WE GOING TO give your Uncle Leon our permission to talk to Blake Tanner about being a donor for Devon?" David asked Vicki. "He needs to have initial tests done to see if he would even be able to be the donor."

"I know, I know. I guess I'm procrastinating because we went to a lot of effort to keep Blake *out* of Devon and Bethany's lives and now I'm having a hard time inviting him back into their lives," she answered.

David stood behind her and massaged her shoulders. "I understand, Honey. It's inconceivable that he was even found, let alone living in a rehab residence where he's evidently doing well. We have to accept it as being a 'God kind of thing,' I believe. Devon needs a kidney, and if Blake is the one to be the donor, so be it. We can't mess around with Devon's life, right?"

"You're right, of course, David. Devon is our first concern. We can deal with everything else after we know the details. One day at a time, correct?"

David dialed Leon's number. "Leon? This is David Marsh. Do you need our written permission to talk to Blake about Devon and taking the blood tests or do you want us to talk to him on the phone?"

"I don't believe I need written permission to ask him. Lucy volunteered to fly out here and talk to him about the entire procedure and what's involved, but you and Victoria are the parents so I'll let you make the call on that one," Leon told him.

"Before anyone flies out there, I think we should speak to Devon's doctor, explain the situation and let him contact a doctor near you. If Blake agrees, he can have the preliminary tests to determine if he's an eligible donor done at a hospital there. Then we can proceed," David suggested.

*   *   *

Cal returned from the retreat excited about the many young people who had been exposed to the gospel of Jesus Christ and the number of them who dedicated or re-dedicated their lives to him. His joy was contagious as he told Lucy about the entire weekend.

"It was enjoyable and inspiring, but I'm happy to know the group's guitarist will be back for next weekend's services," he said. "I might play with them once in a while to give someone a break, but I don't want to be a *regular*. I enjoy worshiping with my family."

He sat on the swing next to Lucy. "So tell me about your weekend, Lucy. You didn't need to have that conversation with Barney, did you?" he laughed.

She smiled at him. "Oh, we had a conversation, for sure, or perhaps, it was more like a confrontation. I think Doug and Jarrod should tell you about Barney."

Cal raised his eyebrows in surprise. "How about you tell me the story and then I'll listen to the boys' version later?"

Lucy filled him in on the search for the boys and how the entire scenario played out.

"You're kidding, right?" he said when she finished. "Have the boys received any consequences for disobeying all the rules?"

"I'm not sure what their punishments are yet. I believe Sean and Paul were hoping to speak to you about the appropriate action. They don't want the boys to be punished just for the sake of punishment but would rather they learn something from the whole experience. I think Ben was the one to suggest they wait for you. He seemed to recall a few consequences from his childhood," she chuckled.

Cal smiled at the thought. "Yeah, I'll bet he does."

He put his arm around her and pulled her to him. "I may have to think about this for a while. They could have been killed or seriously hurt, as well as you and everyone who was in that pasture. They will have to understand the seriousness of their actions; not just that they disobeyed."

"I've been saying a lot of *thank you* prayers, Cal. I want you to know I was fully prepared to shoot Barney, if it became necessary, regardless of bloodlines."

"I would expect no less, Lucy. People and their safety can't be compared to worrying about an animal's bloodlines," he agreed.

"You know, Honey," Lucy continued, "I've been thinking about something else. I really believe the boys are old enough to learn how to shoot. They don't need to own a gun like I did when I was eight-years-old, but I think they need to know how to handle one. The girls, too, but they can wait another couple of years, I think. I'm not sure I can convince Paul and Lynne of that. How do you think Sean and Samantha would feel about it?"

"I think they will probably be okay with it. Samantha has always been around guns and Sean probably has, too. I never see him wearing one, but I would almost certainly bet he owns a few. I guess the subject has never come up so we won't know until we ask. But I suppose it would be prudent to wait until the whole weekend incident is in the past before we talk about the boys and shooting."

"Yes, you're right. By the way, you received a letter from your sister while you were gone. Don't forget...if she says she's coming for a week, I win the wager, even though I don't know what it is," she laughed.

"See what happens when I leave for three days?" Cal asked. "The world at home flies into a million pieces."

"It seems like that's a good reason for you to stay right here, Cowboy, where you can keep it all together," Lucy told him as she kissed him and reminded him she had not seen him for three days.

CHAPTER 17

THE LETTER FROM TESS told him she accepted the invitation to spend a week at the ranch in July. Cal was surprised and, perhaps, even a little excited about seeing her after all the years of no contact.

"What are we going to talk about, Lucy?" he asked. "I have no idea what's going on in her life or what has gone on in the last twenty years. It will be like having a stranger here."

"She is a stranger, so begin with telling her about your life; tell her about your children and grandchildren, and the ranch. You'll find the two of you will remember the years you did spend together as children. It won't be so difficult if you don't make it that way. Follow your instincts, ok?"

"Okay. I'm glad you'll be by my side; you always know what to say."

Lucy shook her head. "Thanks for the compliment but I'm the woman who often speaks first and thinks later, remember, my dear? On that subject, I forgot to tell you, I fired one of your recent hires this past weekend. I was worried about finding the boys and he was wasting precious time with his remarks about not taking orders from a woman. That thoroughly ticked me off, so I fired him...just that fast." She snapped her fingers to indicate how quickly it happened.

Cal considered what she told him. "Okay. You knew what needed to be done and you did it. I trust your decisions, Lucy. Is he coming around for his pay, even if it's only for a week?"

"I suppose. I don't really know; I didn't get that far. I just told him to leave. I believe Len said his name was Stan."

*   *   *

Lucy opened the stall and led Harmony and her foal into the pasture to run and enjoy the sunshine. The grandchildren had many suggestions for the foal's name, everything from Cookie to Batman. They finally all agreed on Fletcher. The two of them were looking healthy and strong. Lucy had been riding Harmony for short periods of time in the pasture by the stable. Fletcher didn't want to let his momma out of his sight, so he ran beside them.

Before she took Harmony's bridle off, she heard voices in the office at the end of the stables. Someone was having a shouting match with Cal, which was totally out of character for him. She decided she would ignore the situation, finish with Harmony and return to the house, when she heard her name mentioned. She couldn't resist the urge to glance through the crack in the door that had been left slightly ajar. Stan was telling Cal he was not going to take orders from a woman, even if she was the boss' wife and he refused to take his paycheck and leave. He insisted there should be severance pay of some sort or he should be allowed to continue working.

"Severance pay?" Cal asked, incredulous at the idea of it. "You were only employed here for a week and you refused to do what my wife told you to do. You're lucky you're receiving the paycheck."

Lucy couldn't see Stan but she could see Cal's face and she couldn't remember seeing him that upset before.

"Well, Mr. Frasier, I got a picture here that might change your mind and make you think twice about going away and leaving your bossy wife in charge, especially with your foreman around. See that? They look pretty cozy, don't they? Hugging each other and all." He held his phone out for Cal to see.

Lucy saw the look on Cal's face before she turned away. She couldn't believe Cal would even consider the fact that she and Len were hugging each other. Then she remembered the group hug the four of them had when they rescued the boys. Where were Sean and Danielle in Stan's picture?

She took Harmony out of her stall, told Fletcher he would have to be lonesome for a while and rode bareback toward the cabin.

She couldn't ride as fast as she wanted because Harmony was not conditioned to it yet. When she was halfway there, she heard hoof beats behind her. Cal caught up with her and grabbed the reins. He dismounted, quickly seized her arms and pulled her off Harmony. He held her at arm's length. "Don't you ever run from me, Lucy Mae. Do you hear me? Never, ever run from me like you just did."

Lucy had never seen Cal angry since she met him, even the night in Illinois when she was pounding his chest with her fists and screaming at him to get out of her house. "Why did you run?" he shouted at her.

"I saw the look on your face when Stan showed you that picture. You were hurt which made me think you believed what he said and you don't trust me," she whispered.

"Do you really think so little of my love for you that you thought I wouldn't know the truth?" He loosened his grip on her arms. "It's not easy to have total trust in someone. To be totally trusted is priceless. That trust should be vigorously protected. I trust you implicitly but you don't trust me, evidently."

"I do trust you, Cal. I couldn't wrap my mind around the fact that you could somehow believe that I would ever do anything improper with another man or do anything to destroy your trust."

He dropped his hands to his side. "I'm sorry if I hurt you just now. I couldn't wrap *my* mind around the fact you were running away from me. What happened to talking to each other before we jump to conclusions?"

Lucy noticed Cal's bruised knuckles and immediately knew how that happened. He must have been unbelievably angry at Stan; she knew it would take a lot for Cal to hit someone.

"Will you come to the cabin with me, Cal?" Lucy asked. "Please."

He shook his head. "I think I'd better get back. You should take Harmony back, too. Fletcher's probably having a fit without her."

Lucy nodded. "You're right. I'll walk her back slowly. You can go ahead."

Lucy had time to think on the slow ride back to the stables. There must still be a shadow of doubt in Cal's mind about that picture. She knew she wasn't mistaken about the look she saw on his face when Stan showed it to him. It made him angry; angrier than she had ever seen him, but was his anger totally about Stan and his accusations or was it partly directed at her for the perceived indiscretion? She wanted to cry but a part of her refused to let her emotions show.

Lucy fixed dinner and they ate in silence. After the kitchen was cleaned, she went to bed. She heard Cal come into the bedroom and was well aware of the fact that he didn't curl his body around hers as he had every night of their married lives. She couldn't stand to lay there without his arm around her. When she was sure he was asleep, she got up, put a robe on and went to the front porch swing. Finally, in the dark, she allowed herself the luxury of tears.

Ben came out of his house and was surprised to see her. "You couldn't sleep either?" he asked.

"No, I guess I have insomnia," she lied. "What are you doing out here, Ben?"

"I wanted a bit of peace. Everyone, including Candy, is asleep so I thought I'd take advantage of it and enjoy some night air."

Lucy hoped it was dark enough he wouldn't notice she'd been crying. "How's Candy coping? Is the group helping?"

Ben said, "She's only been to the mother's group one time but she seemed to feel a little better when she came home. Just realizing that she isn't alone in her feelings was encouraging. She's going to see the counselor next week, about the depression but mainly about dealing with her parents, too."

"Good. I'm glad she is. I hope it helps on so many levels," Lucy told him.

"Are you okay, Lucy?" Ben asked.

"No, not really, but it's nothing you can fix," she said, more to herself than to Ben.

"I'm a pretty good listener, if you need to talk," he offered.

"Thanks but I don't even know what to tell you. Your father and I seem to have a trust issue I didn't know existed until today."

"I'm sorry. Maybe you two need to take off for some island getaway again," he laughed. "I'm sure it will work itself out. I'm going to get some sleep while *all's quiet on the home front*," he said as he went inside.

Lucy drew her knees up and wrapped her arms around them. She put her head down on her arms.

"Is there room on that swing for two people?" Cal asked.

She had not heard him come out of the house and was surprised when she saw him. She nodded and moved over so he could sit beside her. He put his arm around her shoulders and pulled her over to him. "Lucy, I couldn't sleep without you in my arms. Let's talk about this, okay?" he asked.

She nodded. "Who were you really angry with, Cal? Stan, for taking the picture...or me, because you believed what you saw in the picture?"

He sighed, "Maybe a little of both when I first saw it. He caught me off guard. That's when you saw that look on my face. Then I recalled what Ken told us about altered pictures before we left for the retreat. If you had stayed for a minute instead of running away, you would have seen me smash his face for suggesting anything about you, Lucy."

"Would you like me to tell you about the picture?" Lucy asked him.

"You don't have to. I know it was fixed somehow. It doesn't matter, but if you want to, go ahead."

Lucy felt she needed to explain, even if Cal didn't care. "When we found the boys, and successfully got them out of the pasture, we were all relieved. We had a group hug out of sheer elation and exhaustion. Sean and Danielle were in that picture, too, until Stan obviously cropped them out." She turned his face to hers. "You surely know I would never do anything to jeopardize what we have, Cal. I love you with every fiber of my being. I'm sorry for not staying and explaining."

"I don't know how many ways I can say I'm sorry, Lucy, but I am. I can't even imagine you in the arms of another man." He kissed her, then grabbed her hand and pulled her to her feet. "Come on, I have an idea." They ran across the yard in the moonlight.

He brought Cutter out of the stable, swung up on to the big bay's bare back and pulled Lucy up behind him. She put her arms around his waist and they rode to the cabin.

She giggled and said, "We should have left a note. If anyone comes to our door in the morning, they'll think the Rapture occurred and we were taken."

Cal laughed at the thought. "We may enjoy some rapture tonight, Lucy Mae, but not that kind."

Chapter 18

"MOM?" Vicki's voice was barely audible on Lucy's phone.

"Vicki, what's wrong?" Lucy asked, afraid of what she was going to hear.

"Nothing's wrong. I've been crying because I'm deliriously happy and I needed to tell you."

"Great...so what are you so pleased about? Are you and David having another baby?"

Lucy could hear David laughing in the background. "Obviously, I'm on speaker," she observed.

"Yes, you are and no, we aren't having a baby. Devon's doctor called; Blake Tanner is a perfect match for the kidney transplant. He can have all the preliminary tests done at the hospital in Denver. Then he would only need to come to Houston for the actual surgery and recovery time."

"That's the best news I've heard in a while," Lucy said. "Has he agreed to do this? I don't remember you telling me you talked to him about it."

"We did have a conference call with Blake, Uncle Leon, Devon's doctor and the doctor in Denver. Blake was a little hesitant at first. I don't think the surgery frightened him but the stipulations we had in place if he ever had contact with the kids concerned him."

"What happens when he has to travel to Texas? I'm sure the judge who placed him at Mountain House won't agree to allow him to get on a plane by himself."

Vicki answered, "Uncle Leon is working on that right now. If the judge agrees, he will accompany Blake to Texas and stay until he can return to Colorado."

"I'm thrilled this has worked out for Devon. God has definitely answered our prayers about this," Lucy told her. "I'm coming to town to help Phoebe, and I can't wait to tell her, but I'll let Cal know first."

Lucy found Cal and shared Vicki's news. "I'm going to help Phoebe at the shop for a few hours. I'll be back before dinner," she said as she kissed him good-by.

*   *   *

Phoebe and Lucy attacked a few bags of donated clothing that were dropped off that morning. "What are you planning when Cal's sister stays for a week?" Phoebe asked.

"I don't know but I have been thinking about it. I don't want her to be bored to death and I'm afraid she will be. In New York, she probably has many things to occupy her time."

"What kind of work does she do?" Phoebe asked. "Has she been married? What prompted her suddenly to contact Cal?"

Lucy hung a shirt on a hanger, checked the size and placed it on a rack in the proper place. "Your guess is as good as mine, Phoebe," she replied. "I don't have the answers to any of those questions and neither does Cal. Maybe the two of them can spend the week asking questions about each other's lives."

"I know it's been a long time, but they did grow up together, right?" Phoebe asked.

"Yes, until high school, I believe. Then Cal stayed with friends most of the time until he left for college. He and his stepfather didn't see eye to eye on a lot of issues. He spent every summer and any school breaks at the ranch with his dad. Tess preferred the city life so there hasn't been much in common for forty-plus years. It should be an interesting visit. If she gets too bored, maybe I'll bring her in here to volunteer for a day."

They worked and visited for a few more hours. Lucy relayed the good news about Devon's father being a perfect match and told her about Jackie and Gary taking a short vacation before Gary's father moved in with them.

"That's going to be a tough situation for Jackie," Phoebe said. "She will be the main caretaker and she already has her hands full taking care of Gabe and his needs...and Baby Michael."

"I know. I hope they know what they're doing. Even though her father-in-law isn't ill like John was, it's still a huge burden to have to take care of someone. I know they've checked into some services like home health care and visiting nurses. That way, at least, she won't be responsible for bathing and dressing him every day."

"Has Ben's ankle healed? I laughed when I heard he stepped on a Lego, even though I'm sure it was not a laughing matter when it happened," Phoebe confessed.

Lucy smiled, "Yes, he's fine and the twins are getting so chubby. You just want to squeeze them to pieces when you hold them. Are you and Jerry coming for Cal's birthday? Then you can meet Tess *and* squeeze all the babies. It's hard for me to believe Olivia Rose is nearly two and a half, Luke is almost two and Michael is one. They grow so fast."

Phoebe nodded. "Jerry mentioned Cal's birthday but since y'all have had so much going on in the last month, he wasn't sure if you were celebrating or not."

"Phoebe, you have truly become a Texan. I just heard you say, y'all. That's the true indicator," Lucy laughed. "Back to the party...it will be simple this year, no fireworks, just lunch and cake and ice cream. It will serve two purposes: Cal's birthday and everyone meeting Tess. I hope she's not overwhelmed."

Before Lucy left, she asked Phoebe, "Have you heard anything from Anna? She hasn't paid her store rent for two months. I sent her a friendly reminder, but I didn't hear from her. I don't need the rent money, but I would like to know what her plans are for buying the building. If she doesn't want it, I could sell it and be done with all ties to Illinois, except for our annual November holiday trip."

Phoebe shook her head. "I called to give her my number because all I had the day I stopped to see her was one of your cards. I left a message but she hasn't responded. I worry about her."

*   *   *

When Lucy returned, she found a note from Danielle attached to the front door of the house. It read, 'Ms. Frasier, I would like to talk to you. You can call my cell phone when you have time.' *Hmmm, I wonder what that's all about,* Lucy asked herself. She would call her this evening.

*   *   *

When Cal came in, she asked him what he had decided about the boys' consequences.

"I'm going to let them know when they come for my birthday. Sometimes the wait to find out what's going to be meted out is worse than the actual punishment. It gives the transgressor lots of time to think about it," he told her.

There was a message on the answering machine from Tess. She would be arriving tomorrow morning instead of two days later, as originally planned. When Lucy told Cal, he asked if she said anything about renting a car or needing directions to the ranch. She had lived where Paul and Lynne lived now, but she was too little when she moved away to remember how to get there. Lucy suggested he call her and find out. He wrinkled his nose at that suggestion, indicating he really wanted Lucy to do it.

"Calvin Frasier, I declare. You are afraid of your sister. Did she beat you up when you were little or what?" Lucy teased him.

She called the number on the caller ID. "Hello, Tess? This is Lucy, Cal's wife. We got your message about arriving tomorrow. Will you need someone to pick you up or are you planning on renting a car? If you are, I can give you directions on the phone."

'Rent a car? Tess thought. 'I don't have enough money to buy a soda on the plane, I certainly can't afford to rent a car. I knew this was a bad idea. I should never have let Sandi convince me to come.' Aloud, she said, "I guess someone will have to pick me up. I didn't plan on renting a car."

"That's okay, Tess. I'm not sure who will meet you but someone will, I promise. You may have to hold a sign that has your name on it, so they will know who you are," Lucy laughed, although she was serious. "We are all looking forward to this long overdue visit." She smirked at Cal when she said it.

"See, Honey, that wasn't so hard. Now, are you going to have time to pick her up?"

Cal was shaking his head. "Ben and I have business in Magnolia all day tomorrow. Can you do it?"

"No, I can't. I told Candy I would watch all three babies while she goes to her mothers' group. I do not want her to miss it; she needs it. This is crazy. If Tess hadn't changed her flight, this wouldn't be a problem."

"I think I'll ask Len to do it," Cal said. "She might as well meet a real cowboy the minute she reaches Texas."

Lucy rolled her eyes at his last statement. "If you want Len to pick her up, you need to call him tonight. I think he starts working at the crack of dawn. Tell him he can take my car. That's better for a first impression than the beater truck he drives."

* * *

After dinner, Lucy called the number Danielle had given her. She listened to the hesitant request Danielle was making and smiled. "Yes, Honey, I will be happy to help you with that. Mr. Frasier's sister is coming for a visit, so we might have to wait until she leaves to go shopping. Will that be okay?"

"What was that all about?" Cal asked as they got ready for bed.

"Just girl stuff. You wouldn't understand," she laughed.

"I don't know about that," Cal said. "I think I understand girl stuff pretty well, at least, if it's about *my* girl," he whispered in her ear as he snuggled up to her.

She rolled over to look at him. "You're absolutely right. You do understand me so well. It's almost scary at times, but I love it. You know what to do or say to make me laugh, to cheer me up if I'm sad, to console me or to make me feel cherished. You are a rare man, Calvin B. Frasier and I thank God every day for putting you in my life."

Cal kissed her before he said, "I'm not sure I can live up to all that praise, but you forgot to say I was a good lover, too."

Lucy smiled at him, ran her fingers through his hair and whispered, "I know it's true, Cowboy, but I think we should do a little more research on that."

CHAPTER 19

"LUCY," CAL CALLED. "Where are you?" He continued through the house until he reached their master bathroom. He heard the shower suddenly shut down. Assuming she needed her towel, he pulled the shower curtain aside and held the towel out to her.

"Jeepers," Lucy exclaimed as she jumped back. "You scared me, Cal."

He laughed at her. "Who did you think it was? There's no one here but me."

She took the towel and wrapped it around her. "Have you noticed we have an extraordinary number of conversations in the bathroom?"

"As many people as we have coming and going in our house, it seems to be the only place for a private conversation," Cal observed.

"Why were you looking for me? I thought you had already left. Did you forget something?"

Cal took a deep breath and exhaled slowly. "If Ben wasn't waiting for me, I would be happy to show you what I forgot...but since he is, I will forgo that pleasure. I came to tell you Annie has called twice wondering when you'll be there to pick her up and I wanted to let you know everything is set for Len to pick Tess up from the airport."

Lucy nodded. "I'll call Annie to tell her I'm on my way, in a few minutes. She's going to help me with Luke and the twins today. I don't think I can manage all three of them by myself. How are Len and Tess going to find each other?" Lucy had a mental picture of Len, probably the most reticent man she knew and one who hated crowds, going into the airport to look for a woman he had never met.

"I took a picture of Len, at gunpoint, almost," Cal laughed "and sent it to the number Tess gave us. I hope it all works out."

"Will you be home in time to grill some steaks? I'll prepare the rest and Len can eat with us, too. Poor guy," she said, shaking her head.

Cal kissed her and left. "I'll see you this afternoon. I love you, Lucy."

She watched him go and thanked God he had not seen her face right before he entered the bathroom when she discovered the lump in her right breast while doing her usual once-a-month self-exam. She didn't know yet how she was going to tell him. Since his first wife, Kathy, died of breast cancer, Cal would be devastated to even think about the possibility.

*   *   *

She brought Annie back and went to Candy's house. Luke came running to meet them, talking all the way.

"Shhh, Luke," Candy told him. "Remember, Mommy said we have to use our inside voices when the babies are sleeping."

Lucy grinned at her as the words rolled off his back. "I'm not sure that isn't Luke's inside voice," she told Candy.

Candy nodded, acknowledging that truth, and then proceeded to show Lucy where the bottled breast milk was kept in the refrigerator. She had all the instructions written down.

When Annie took Luke to his room to pick out some toys to play with, Candy asked Lucy, "Do you think it would be possible for you to watch the children at your house on Thursday evening? I'll bring everything they need and they're usually only waking up once a night now."

"Yes, sure, Candy. Are you and Ben going out for the evening?"

Candy blushed, making her freckles stand out even more. "Not exactly. I thought I would surprise Ben with a nice dinner and we would spend the evening at home. He's been so patient and worked very hard at taking care of me and the kids, too."

Lucy smiled at her pretty red-haired daughter-in-law. "I think that's a wonderful idea, Candy. You and Ben deserve some time alone. I'm very pleased you're feeling better."

Candy nodded. "The mother's group has helped me sort through the depressed feelings. I still drop off the edge sometimes, but not nearly as often. I can even fit into a couple pair of my pre-baby jeans."

"Good for you, although I'm certain Ben wouldn't care if you ever fit into them, Candy. Now get out of here. Annie and I will hold down the fort."

* * *

For being born several weeks early, Sophia and Samuel were unusually good sleepers. Lucy and Annie soon had it down to a science: change them, feed them, burp them and they went right back to sleep with only a short time to hold them and try to coax a smile from them. Luke, on the other hand, was a whirlwind of perpetual motion. He eventually fell asleep for his nap, too.

"Well, Annie, what do you think of taking care of babies? Someday, you may have your own to take care of," Lucy told her.

"Well, I'm going to order mine one at a time, Grammy," she said so earnestly, Lucy laughed out loud.

Lucy stewed all day about how she would tell Cal about the lump she found. She couldn't keep her hand from feeling for it, hoping it was her imagination this morning, but it was always there.

*   *   *

Candy came home, with Cal and Ben arriving shortly after. "Where's Tess?" Cal asked. "And Len?"

Lucy shrugged her shoulders. "I haven't heard from anyone. Maybe they're still wandering around in the airport looking for each other," she laughed.

Cal frowned. "You don't suppose they really are still searching for each other, do you?"

"Why don't you call Tess and find out? I put the salad together this afternoon in Candy's kitchen. Ben and Candy, will you join us? Your father thinks the more people, the better, so he won't have to talk to Tess so much," she teased him, swatting him on his rump as she walked by.

"I'm going to clean up and put the steaks on the grill," Cal said, ignoring her remark. "I hope they arrive in time to eat."

As Lucy passed through the great room, she glanced out the large windows. "Isn't that my car at the guest house?" she asked Cal. "I think Len found her and delivered her to her house without stopping here."

"Annie, call your mother and see if you can stay, too. I don't have time to take you home right now. Or better yet, ask them to come eat with us," Lucy told her.

As Lucy took the steaks to Cal at the grill, Len walked up the steps onto the patio, with Tess. Lucy wasn't sure she recognized Len. Obviously, the man did own some clothes and boots other than the ones he wore to work cattle. Cal turned to this stranger with Len and couldn't decide if he should hug her or shake hands with her. Lucy couldn't stand the tension. "Tess, how nice to meet you. I'm Lucy, Cal's wife," she said as she walked toward the woman who looked nothing like Cal.

She gave her a hug. "I hope y'all had a good flight and that you're hungry, because your brother knows how to grill a steak to perfection," she continued. "Len, we want you to stay, too."

Tess was smiling but couldn't take her eyes off Cal. "Well, big brother, you're just as handsome as you ever were," she told him. She walked over and wrapped her arms around him. He finally found his voice and told her, "Tess, you look exactly as I remember you."

She laughed at that. "Not much taller, but a lot wider, huh?"

After the initial introductions, conversation flowed freely during dinner. Paul, Lynne and Jarrod came for dessert and took Annie home with them. Ben and Candy took their family home, also. Len said he should be going, too. That's when Tess asked if he would mind walking her home to the guest house since it was dark.

Lucy raised an eyebrow to Cal and he shook his head at her. She watched them leave and considered how different Tess and Cal seemed. Cal was obviously very tall and lean while Tess was quite short and stout. She was talkative, much more so than Cal but maybe she was nervous tonight.

They discussed the day while Cal helped her clean up. "She looks exactly like our mother. I think that's why I was dumbstruck when I first saw her," Cal told Lucy. "She seems to have a much nicer personality than our mother did, though."

Lucy didn't question that statement, knowing he would tell her what he meant, when he was ready to share. Cal rarely mentioned his mother. He obviously enjoyed and respected his father much more.

*   *   *

They watched a program or two on television when Cal finally said, "Lucy, what are you doing? You've been feeling your side all evening. Does it hurt?"

She shook her head but didn't offer an explanation.

When they got into bed, she couldn't keep from telling him any longer. Their relationship was based on trust and truth; she didn't want to jeopardize that but she knew the pain it was going to cause him.

"Cal, I have to tell you something. I found a lump in my right breast this morning when I did my monthly exam."

All color drained from his face. He stared at her in disbelief. When he found his voice, he asked, "How long were you going to wait until you told me?"

"I wish I didn't have to tell you at all. I knew how this was going to affect you. But remember, Honey, this could easily be just a lump. Women have lumpectomies every day with no malignancy. Please don't jump to conclusions."

"Did you make a doctor's appointment?" he asked with tears in his eyes.

Lucy nodded. "Yes, this morning. I go for an initial exam tomorrow morning. There was a cancellation, so they gave me the appointment."

Cal nodded. "What time? I'll go with you."

"Why don't you stay here and get to know your sister? This is just an appointment with my doctor, no tests or anything yet."

Cal stood and walked away, then turned to her and quietly said, "I will go with you, Lucy. I don't care who is here. Tess can entertain herself or watch television all day for all I care."

He held her so tightly in bed, she almost couldn't breathe, but she fell asleep that way.

* * *

When she woke in the morning, Cal was not by her. She smelled coffee so she knew he was up, wandering around somewhere.

She found him on the glider on the patio, with his forearms on his knees, hands folded and his head bowed. She knew he was praying earnestly and it broke her heart for him. When she went to him, he sat up and indicated she should sit next to him. She placed her head on his shoulder.

"Don't push me away, Lucy. Please don't do that."

"I don't understand, Cal," she told him. "Why do you think I would do that?"

He spoke so softly, she could hardly hear him. "Kathy pushed me away when she knew she had cancer. She wouldn't allow me to go to any appointments or treatments with her. I believe she transferred her anger at the disease to me. It was hard; I vowed I would not be pushed away again. I will not be a bystander, Lucy. I won't sit in waiting rooms and read six-month-old magazines. I will be wherever you are and no one will stop me."

"I want you with me on this journey, wherever it leads us, Cal. I promise I will not push you away. I want you by my side; you are my strength."

Cal called Tess and left a message explaining there was a doctor's appointment but they would be back soon. Perhaps they would return before she got up. He didn't know if she was a late sleeper or not.

* * *

When the nurse called Lucy's name, she and Cal both went back to the examining room. The nurse looked at Cal strangely when she told Lucy to disrobe, as though she was waiting for him to leave the room. Lucy smiled at her and said, "It's okay. He's seen my breasts before today."

The doctor came in, looked at Cal standing next to where Lucy was laying and holding her hand. She smiled at him, "I like a man who supports his wife," she said.

Her exam confirmed what Lucy had found. There definitely was a lump. "You will need to have a mammogram and possibly, an ultrasound, depending on what the mammogram shows. I'll have the scheduler see how soon she can get an appointment for you."

Cal spoke up, "I want it done this week."

The doctor shook her head. "I doubt that will be possible, Mr. Frasier. These mammograms are usually scheduled out a few weeks; however, due to the nature of this particular lump, I will request the earliest possible appointment. Perhaps there will be a cancellation and it can be done sooner." Without further conversation, she started to leave the room.

Cal blocked her path to the door. "What do you mean by, *the nature of this particular lump?*" he asked.

She told them that lumps in breasts have different 'feels' and while it certainly isn't conclusive, she felt this lump should be looked at as soon as possible.

On their way home, Lucy suggested, "Let's not tell everyone about this until we know more, okay, Honey? I understand your need to talk to someone, maybe Pastor Kelly or Jerry, but I don't want to ruin Tess' visit or anyone else's plans. We'll pray about an earlier appointment and let God handle the details, okay?"

Cal smiled at her and nodded his head in agreement. *'If she only knew how many days and nights I spent on my knees begging God to spare Kathy's life,'* he thought.

Chapter 20

TESS OPENED HER EYES and looked around. For a few seconds, she couldn't remember where she was. Then the events of yesterday came flooding back into her memory. She rolled onto her back and thought of the scene at the airport when the somewhat scruffy, handsome cowboy was scrutinizing every female passenger to see if they recognized him, since he didn't have a picture of her. He looked so uncomfortable, the memory of it made her laugh.

She made a cup of tea for herself and opened cupboards to see what was available for breakfast. She wished her cupboards at home had this much food in them…and this was the guesthouse. Calvin must certainly be doing well. She liked his pretty wife, Lucy. She seemed friendly and down-to-earth. His son, Ben, was a mountain of a man, tall, broad shouldered and as handsome as they come. He looked so much like Calvin, who looked like he was fifty instead of sixty-something and he definitely looked like their father. It was no wonder their mother had fallen in love with him. It made her sad to think her parents couldn't stay together. She believed her mother never stopped loving her father but her pride wouldn't allow her to go back to Texas once she left. That's probably what turned her into a bitter old woman; that, and the cruel man she married.

Tess listened to her phone message. Calvin said Lucy had a doctor's appointment. It must have been important because he said yesterday he was going to show her some of the ranch today. She certainly hoped he didn't mean on horseback.

She ate some cereal, took her tea and went outside. It wasn't too hot yet but maybe that was because it was still morning. As she was contemplating what to do this morning, Len rode up to the yard on his horse.

"Good mornin' ma'am," he said as he touched the brim of his hat. It was like a picture out of an old western movie and Tess would have laughed if she wouldn't have hurt his feelings.

"Please call me, Tess. None of this 'ma'am' stuff. Okay, Len?"

He smiled at her. "Okay, Tess. Ben sent me over to see if there was anything you needed this morning before the boss and Lucy came back."

"I've already eaten a bowl of cereal, but thanks," she told him. She thought he looked disappointed. "I think I'll just hang out for a while. I'm sure they'll be back soon."

"All right. I have to get to work. Maybe I'll see you again before you go back to New York." He rode off toward the barns she could see in the distance.

Back to New York...what was there for her? An apartment she wouldn't be able to pay for in another month, no job, no car, and no income. How would she ever have enough nerve to beg Calvin to let her stay? Did she really want to stay? No, but where else was she going to go? This was making her head hurt. She decided to go back to bed.

*   *   *

Lucy knocked on the door to the guesthouse. When Tess answered, she asked, "Would you like to have lunch with me and my best friend in the world? She would love to meet you. After lunch, we can do some window shopping, if you'd like and stroll around the town of Magnolia."

Tess agreed, although she wasn't a fan of window shopping. She liked the real kind of shopping. Unfortunately, her resources didn't allow that any longer.

During lunch, they discussed the advantages of living in a big city. Phoebe told Tess she had lived in or near Chicago her entire life and Lucy filled her in on her many years in Chicago, also.

"So, how did you adjust to Texas?" Tess inquired. "I can't even imagine the culture shock of moving here."

Phoebe and Lucy both laughed. "Actually, Texas isn't devoid of culture, Tess. We have all the amenities of other big cities, even though it may not be evident when you're out on the ranch, away from everything," Lucy explained. "I chose to move back because the love of my life lived here and I would have moved to Africa if he had asked me to."

Phoebe nodded. "We need to find you a good Texas man, Tess, because that's the reason I left Chicago, too. I would have followed Jerry anywhere."

Tess laughed at them. "I don't think I will find a man in a week," she added.

"I don't know..." Lucy teased. "I think Len is pretty smitten with you, Tess."

Tess blushed all shades of pink and shook her head at these two women. She liked both of them. She didn't have any good friends in New York; there were a few acquaintances, but not good friends.

Lucy became serious and asked, "Tess, if you don't mind, tell me about Cal's childhood. He never speaks of it. He talks about his high school and college years but nothing before that."

Tess seemed a bit uncomfortable. "I was very young when Mom took us back to New York. Calvin was a few years older and I know he didn't want to leave our father or the ranch. He talked about how he was going back when he was old enough.

Mom would punish him every time he mentioned it. After she married Nick, things got worse for Calvin. They definitely didn't like each other. Nick would slap him around if he even mentioned Dad or Texas. There came a day when Calvin was bigger and stronger than Nick. He warned Nick not to push him around again, but Nick wouldn't listen. Calvin hit him and walked out. He never really came back. He lived with some good friends from high school and, of course, came to the ranch every chance he got. Nick was not abusive in any way to me or my mother, just to Calvin. He looked like Dad and I suppose Nick thought he was a constant reminder of Mom's former life." Tess stared out the window; then continued, "I don't think Mom ever stopped loving my father and I don't think Calvin ever forgave her for leaving Texas and then not protecting him from Nick. I don't know, but I am very happy to see Calvin happy and he doesn't seem to bear any scars from those years. He seems to be a good father and husband."

Lucy wiped some tears from her eyes. She reached over the table and took Tess' hand. "Thank you for sharing that with me, Tess. You have no idea what a good, loving and godly man your brother is."

They wandered around the streets of Magnolia before heading back to the ranch and dinner.

*   *   *

Cal and Tess reminisced about some of the good times they remembered. "Do you remember, Calvin, when Mom paid for some guitar lessons for you? We were ready to buy ear plugs before you finally learned a few chords that didn't sound like nails on a chalkboard."

He smiled. "Yes, I do remember. I wanted to learn so badly. I was going to have my own country western band, I thought." He turned to her and asked, "Tess, can I ask a favor of you? Will you call me Cal instead of Calvin, please? Calvin brings back some forgotten memories for me. Lucy calls me Calvin occasionally and I don't mind, but when you say it, I hear Mom and Nick."

"Of course, Calv..Cal. I'm sorry. I never thought of that. I will try to remember," she promised.

"I would like to show you some of the ranch tomorrow, and the horses and cattle we breed. Did you bring some jeans with you, Tess?" Cal asked her.

"Slacks, yes...but jeans, no. And I guarantee you, Lucy's won't fit me," she laughed. "And please tell me, we aren't going sightseeing on horseback, are we?"

Cal tilted his head at her. "That would be the best way, but I suppose we could ride the ATVs. Would that be better?"

"I don't even know what that is, but I'll give it a try, as long as it's not a horse."

"Tess, I think you need to at least get on a horse before you leave, even if only for a few minutes. I know someone who would probably love to help you with that," Lucy said.

"Lucy, stop playing Cupid," Cal told her with a wink.

Getting a bit more serious, he asked Tess, "So, tell us, what do you do in New York? For a living, I mean."

Tess took a deep breath, thinking it was now or never. "I lost my job due to the company down-sizing and anyone over forty years old was suddenly unemployed. I received a small severance package, but I used it, of course, for rent and other necessities. I don't own a car which is true of most New Yorkers. There's no place to park one and it's easier to grab a cab or use the subway. I've sold most of my possessions to continue to pay my rent on my apartment, but I only have enough left for one more month and then I'm not sure what I'll do. Look for some rich sugar daddy, I guess," she joked, but had tears in her eyes.

Cal and Lucy looked at each other in shock. "Are you telling me the money I paid you for your half of the ranch is all gone?" Cal asked, incredulously. "I'm not judging you, Tess, but that was a sizable chunk of change."

She hung her head and quietly said, "Yes, I know. I have a terrible habit of mismanaging money and spending like there's no tomorrow. But 'tomorrow' eventually comes, doesn't it?"

She excused herself and said she would go to the guest house now.

"Wait, Tess," Cal told her. "It's okay, we'll figure out something. Let's sleep on it and pray about it." He put his arms around her and genuinely hugged her for the first time since she arrived.

*   *   *

As she lay in bed, Tess wondered how to pray about the situation. Prayer in her life stopped when she left Texas at two years of age. Up until then, one of her parents said bedtime prayers with her every night. After they moved, she never heard her mother pray again.

CHAPTER 21

IN THE MORNING, Cal showed Tess how to drive one of the ATVs. She lurched around the yard and the drive until she caught on. While Cal took Tess on a tour, the phone seemed to ring incessantly.

The scheduler for the imaging center said Lucy could come for a mammogram the next day if 8 am wasn't too early.

Vicki called and said there was a problem with the judge allowing Leon to bring Blake to Houston when it was time for the surgery in several months. She was nearly hysterical thinking something could possibly mess with the plans for Devon's life-saving operation.

Jackie wanted to know the dates that would be best for her and Gary to make plans for their weekend getaway while Cal and Lucy watched the boys.

Sean called to speak to Cal about Doug's consequences for the disobedience of a few weeks ago and how they could arrange for him to be at the ranch every day while he fulfilled his obligations.

Lucy was still reeling from what Tess told them last night and trying to think of some sort of solution. She decided to walk to the bunkhouse to speak to Dolores and Alisha about food for the family get-together planned to take place before Tess left. Perhaps walking would clear her head and give her some insight into all of the family's concerns.

Ben was coming out of his house the same time she was. "Good morning, Ben. I'm headed to the bunkhouse to speak to Alisha. Where are you going?"

"I'm going there, too, to talk to Toby. What advice do you think I should give him?"

Lucy looked at Ben, confused. "I'm talking to Alisha about sandwiches; what the heck are you talking about?"

Ben started laughing and explained, "I forgot you don't know the story concerning Alisha and Toby. I was looking for some female advice in the 'love' department."

He proceeded to explain the incident that happened weeks ago. "Now Toby wants to ask her for a date but is scared to death. He's afraid to get close enough to say hello for fear he'll frighten her."

Lucy frowned. "Are you sure he is safe, Ben? He won't let his testosterone get carried away again?"

"No, I'm certain he's got his head screwed on straight now. I've had some long talks with him about women, in general, and how a man treats a woman. He's really just a kid and he never had a decent example of that."

"You truly are a man after your father's heart, Ben. He's a good man in all areas of his life and you are, too. I'll talk to Alisha without really mentioning Toby and see how she feels, okay?"

After Lucy arranged for Dolores and Alisha to make cold sandwiches for the unofficial party because she was too overwhelmed at the moment to do it herself, she asked Alisha if she found the books Lucy had given her.

"Yes, Ben brought them to me, but it was such a crazy day, I forgot about them for a week," Alisha told her.

"Really?" Lucy asked, sounding surprised. "A crazy day in the bunkhouse? That seems a bit odd. It's usually pretty calm in here unless it's time to eat."

Alisha hesitated, as if deciding whether to divulge the story or not. Finally, she told Lucy what happened with Toby. "I do like him, Mrs. Frasier, but I don't know how to let him know. I think he's so embarrassed, he won't even look at me."

"With your permission, Alisha, I'll let Ben handle this. Maybe he can convince Toby you won't carve him up into little pieces if he comes close to you."

* * *

When Cal and Tess returned, Tess looked as if she had ridden a thousand miles. She was a bit disheveled and stiff. "I'm going to take a hot bath, if you don't mind," she told Cal. "I believe you picked the roughest trails you could find, Brother Dear." With that, she limped to the guesthouse.

Lucy put her arms around Cal's waist. "You did that to her on purpose, didn't you, Love?" she asked him.

He grinned at her, "She needs to toughen up a little if she's going to be a Texan."

"Be a Texan?" Lucy asked. "What does that mean?"

"I'll tell you tonight when we have more time and we're alone. How was your day?"

"I spent a lot of time putting out fires...or starting them, I'm not sure which," Lucy told him. "I tried to help get Alisha and Toby back on track, I talked to Leon about the problem of getting Blake here on a commercial plane, I made a time to go shopping with Danielle because she wants to look like a girl for one of your ranch hands, I decided on the food for the party, we need to choose a weekend we can stay with Jackie's boys, and Sean wants to know how to keep Doug here for his consequences and..." she couldn't finish because Cal kissed her, long and hard.

"That was nice," she told him as they separated.

"It was the only way I knew to get you to stop talking," Cal said.

"The most important thing I have to tell you is I have to be at the imaging center at 8'o'clock tomorrow morning. Someone cancelled their appointment."

Cal held her close. There were so many things going on in their lives and the only thing he really cared about was the woman in his arms.

*   *   *

True to his promise, Cal invaded the room where the mammogram was done and once again, Lucy assured the technician he was quite familiar with her breasts and it would be okay for him to be there, although he needed to step behind the protective barrier when the actual pictures were taken. After the radiologist looked at the films, it was decided she did need the ultrasound also, to achieve a more definitive location of the lump. They found a coffee bar until it was time for the ultrasound.

Cal sat beside the table during the ultrasound and held her hand. When he noticed a tear run down the side of her face, he wiped it off with his rough hand. She turned her head to him and for the first time since she discovered the lump, she said, "I'm frightened, Cal."

It was almost more than he could bear to see her cry, but telling her everything was going to be okay wasn't what she needed to hear either. "I'm not going to leave your side, Lucy...ever."

The radiologist would confer with her doctor and the surgeon to determine when the initial surgery could be done and someone would call her.

* * *

Lucy was quiet on the drive home. Finally, she declared, "I hate waiting. I want to do this tomorrow and see what the results are. I feel like the boys awaiting their punishment. Nothing moves forward until the wait is over."

"Did you share this with Phoebe or any of the kids?" Cal asked her.

"No, I didn't. Just you, Cal. I don't want a bunch of people fussing over me until we know what we're dealing with. I just need you."

"Phoebe may know since I spoke to Jerry about it, although he's accustomed to keeping confidences."

"You never told me last night what you were talking about when you said Tess needed to learn to be a Texan."

"I wanted to discuss it with you first, but we have much more important things to think about right now. I think we should cancel this party, though. I'm going to have a tough time acting happy."

Lucy shook her head. "Nope. We're going to enjoy the children and grandchildren all getting to meet their Aunt Tess. It will be a diversion for our thoughts."

He nodded. "When are we watching Ben and Candy's children?"

"Tonight," she responded. "Now that should *really* be a diversion," she said, chuckling.

* * *

Candy brought the necessary food and supplies for the three children in the afternoon. There was already a crib in the spare bedroom for Luke, but she brought a portable crib for the twins to sleep in. "I can never tell you how much I appreciate this, Lucy. Please tell Cal that, also."

Lucy hugged her and told her to go home and enjoy her evening with Ben, although she was pretty sure they were going to enjoy their evening without her urging.

* * *

Candy prepared a meal and lit the candles she had placed on the dinner table. When Ben came in the door, his eyes reflected his surprise.

"Candy?" he called. She came from the kitchen and put her arms around his neck. "What's all this?" he asked indicating the table with the candles and nice china.

"I haven't made a real meal since the babies were born, Ben. I wanted to show you how much I appreciate you. I know it's been difficult for both of us, but I think my hormones are back in their proper order again and the mother's group therapy has been wonderful for me. I feel like my normal pre-pregnant self again...almost."

He held her at arm's length and told her she looked gorgeous. Then he pulled her close and kissed her. "Mmmm, are the kids asleep?" he asked between kisses.

"They're at your dad's house for the night, Ben. We are actually alone for the first time in two years, I think."
***They enjoyed their meal while they discussed grown-up topics without any interruptions, although neither one of them could concentrate on what they were discussing or eating; they couldn't take their eyes off each other.

Candy told him she had also made his favorite dessert.

"I'm sure that can wait for a while, Baby," he told her as he blew out the candles, picked her up and carried her to their bedroom. "*You* are actually my favorite dessert."

Ben pulled the ribbon from her hair and allowed her red curls to fall on her shoulders. "I've missed you, Candy," he said, his voice husky with emotion. "Not just our intimacy, but our sharing and being together without interruptions."

"I know, Ben. I've missed it too although I wasn't aware of how much until I started feeling better," Candy told him as she unbuttoned his shirt. "I could hardly wait for you to come home today."

*   *   *

Between feedings, Cal discussed his plan with Lucy. "Tess obviously has nothing," he said. "She as much as said so when she admitted she spent every dime and now has no source of income, either. I thought we could rent an apartment for her and provide her with a used vehicle. We can afford to support her until she finds a job. The deal would be she needs to continue counseling...here...for her spending habits and take a few money management courses. Maybe she could also help out with babysitting for Ben and Candy occasionally."

"Spoken like a grandpa holding two babies at once," Lucy laughed. She took Sophia from him and handed him a bottle for Samuel. Luke was playing on the floor by their feet.

"So what do you think? Should we make her the offer? She can go back to New York and think it over and then return if she agrees. I don't see any other solution and she is my sister. I can't let her be homeless, especially since we've been blessed with so much."

"I agree, Cal. Do you think she will accept the offer? She has a lot of pride I think, and she may still hate the thought of living in Texas."

"We won't know until we ask her. Perhaps we should call her right now and have her come over; if she can still walk," he chuckled.

He switched Samuel to his shoulder and dialed Tess's number. When he asked her if she could come over, she said she would as soon as she got home. "What do you mean?

Where are you, Tess?"

"I'm in a town called Cypress. Len invited me to get a burger with him and since I was too sore to fix anything...thanks to you...I accepted his offer. We'll be there in a little while."

"The look on your face is priceless, Cal, and I don't even know what she told you."

"She's with Len," he said. "He invited her for dinner. Maybe it won't be so hard to convince her to stay, after all."

*   *   *

"When are you going back to New York?" Len asked Tess.

"My flight is Sunday, early afternoon," she answered. "Are you taking me to the airport, Len? It seems only right, since you're the one who picked me up when I got here," she flirted.

Len seemed embarrassed. "I don't know. Ms. Frasier loaned me her car to pick you up. If I take you back, it would probably have to be in my old truck."

"That's okay with me," she laughed. "Any transportation will do, as long as it's not one of Cal's ATV things."

They shared a chuckle about her day of riding one of those. "I was so sore that night."

Len cleared his throat and said, quietly, "I wish you weren't leaving, Tess."

CHAPTER 22

THE DAY OF THE PICNIC ARRIVED, along with all the grown-ups and the grandchildren. It was a beautiful day and Tess was overwhelmed with so many names to try and remember.

When Lucy saw Toby helping Alisha bring the food to the main house, she nodded in their direction and whispered to Ben, "Obviously, she didn't kill him."

* * *

Cal took Jarrod and Doug with him to the stables. "It's time you boys find out how well a pitchfork fits your hands," he told them. "Starting next week, I expect you to be up early, cleaning every stall in the stables; not just the stables close to the house, but the ones where the guys keep their horses, too. I know it's a lot of work and possibly more punishment than you feel you deserve, but your actions could have had deadly consequences. Do you realize that?"

They both nodded their heads. "Yes, Sir." They said in unison.

"Doug, your Aunt Lynne and Uncle Paul have agreed to allow you to stay for the week with Jarrod. You boys can ride the ATVs back and forth, with your helmets on, but you are responsible to do your work first before you make any enjoyable plans for the day. Do we understand each other?"

Again, they nodded and answered, "Yes, Sir, Grandpa."

"Okay, then let's go back to the party," Cal said as he put an arm around each boy's shoulders.

*   *   *

"Dad," Samantha called. "We have something for you. It's from all of us, but you have to go inside for a minute while the guys unload it."

Cal went inside while glancing at Lucy. She shrugged her shoulders, indicating she had no idea what it was.

The men unloaded a free-standing hammock. It was the largest one available. They called Cal back out. "Since you're getting so old, we thought you could use some time, *just-a-swingin*," Jackie told him, laughing.

Vicki showed him the name on the tag. "It's called a Canoodling Hammock, Cal, so I guess you and Mom will have to try canoodling in it; as if you two need an excuse to do that," she added. Everyone laughed about that statement.

Cal took a bit to get his long legs in it. "I'm not sure I even know what canoodling is, but come over here, Lucy and we'll give it a try."

"Canoodling is an old word for snuggling or cuddling. I imagine two people in there would have to enjoy snuggling because the weight of one would cause the other one to roll against them. A good name for your hammock, Cal," Lucy chuckled.

She held onto the side and attempted to get into it gracefully. "Obviously, this is meant for someone more coordinated than me," she announced.

"Grandpa, I'll *noodle* with you," Bethany said, as she climbed in easily. Cal hugged her as she lay tightly up against him.

Cake and ice cream was ready for everyone, before the families headed for home.

*   *   *

When only Cal and Lucy and Tess were left on the porch, Tess said, "You are so rich in family, Cal. You have a beautiful wife, children, step-children and grandchildren who love and respect you. I'm so proud of you. Despite everything you endured during childhood, you have a wonderful life and family. I have to say I am extremely jealous and ashamed I waited so long to meet all of them."

With his arms around Lucy, he told her, "We are blessed, for sure, Tess. God has kept us in his care and showered us with more than we deserve, especially since we sinners deserve nothing but his wrath. Lucy and I have an invitation for you. We'd like to share some of our blessings with you, and this tribe you saw tonight is *your* family, too." He proceeded to outline their offer, allowing her time to think about it. "You return to New York and when you're ready to decide, let us know. We'll pay to get your things here, if that's what you choose. This isn't a bribe, it's just an offer. You have to make the decision yourself with no pressure from us."

Tess wiped tears from her eyes and thanked them for offering the help. "I'm going to bed and see if perhaps I remember how to pray. I'll ask God for help making this decision."

Cal took his boots off and climbed back into the hammock. He took Lucy's hand and helped her in also. She rolled against him instantly. They laughed as it was nearly impossible to push away from each other. "This could be a dangerous thing when the grandchildren are old enough to date," Lucy giggled. She finally gave up trying to breathe while being smashed into his side and instead lay with her head on his chest and most of her body on top of his. Cal encircled her with his arms to keep her from rolling off.

*   *   *

They fell asleep that way and that's where Ben found them in the morning. He took a picture with his phone, and then sent it to all four of the adult children, with the caption: "I believe Dad's enjoying his gift."

Lucy opened her eyes and groaned from being in the same position all night. She tilted her head back to look at Cal who was smiling at her. "Mornin' Sleepyhead," he said

"How long have you been awake and why didn't you wake me?" she asked.

"I didn't want to disturb you, Sweetheart. You looked so peaceful."

"Numb might be a better word," she told him. "I really did not intend to sleep out here all night."

"I think it was quite comfortable. Maybe we should move this hammock into our bedroom and replace our bed," Cal said.

"Yeah?" Lucy asked. "Well, listen, Cowboy, you just envision what our romantic nights might be like in this thing, okay?"

Cal laughed at her. "We should always be open to new experiences, I think."

"You're impossible," Lucy told him while trying to climb out of the hammock.

Cal pulled her back in. "Wait a minute, Lucy. I want to talk to you about something."

"Talking before coffee? This must be serious."

Cal brushed the wayward strands of hair off her face and tucked them behind her ear. "I believe it's time we tell our children about your upcoming surgery. We can use all their prayers and while I respect your reasoning of not wanting them to worry, they deserve to know."

Lucy shook her head slightly and commented, "I don't really want to, but I will leave that decision up to you, Cal. I respect your wisdom."

* * *

He called Jackie and Samantha first, knowing they would be devastated for Lucy but also for him, remembering their mother's battle. He stopped at Paul and Lynne's house to tell them in person. Their faces registered their shock and concern for Lucy and for him. Then he drove to Cypress to tell Vicki. She immediately cried and hugged him. "I'm so sorry for you to have to go through this again, Cal, and I can't imagine what Mom's going through. She didn't say anything yesterday at your party."

"She doesn't want you to worry about her, Vicki. She wasn't planning on telling anyone until the initial surgery was done."

"That damned independent streak she has," Vicki said quietly.

"Yes, I know," Cal agreed. "I convinced her to let me tell you. Please pray about it. It may be benign and all this worrying will be for nothing."

Cal dropped in to see Jerry while he was in Cypress. "Did you mention Lucy's surgery to Phoebe?"

Jerry shook his head. "I started to say something several times, but decided I would let Lucy share that with her. Phoebe will probably be furious with me for not telling her but she'll get over it. How are you holding up, Cal?"

"I pray about it constantly but we go about our days as though it isn't *the elephant in the room*." Cal held his hat in his hand. "Jerry, I think I would truly die if anything happened to Lucy. I have never felt for anyone what I feel for her. She truly is my life and the very air I breathe."

Jerry put his arm around Cal's shoulders, although he had to stretch to reach them. "I know, my friend. I know she is. I'll tell Phoebe today so we can pray about it together."

*　*　*

His trip to Cypress didn't take long. He found Ben when he got home and asked if he wanted to go for a short ride. "I know your rides always have a purpose, Dad. What is it this time?" he laughed.

They rode for a while in silence. Cal could hardly get the words out to his son who was the closest of his children. "I realize we don't know the end results yet, but I needed to tell you so you can lift this entire situation up in prayer."

Ben told Cal, "I liked Lucy from the first day I met her, Dad. Remember when you went riding and I brought the horses to Magnolia for you? I could tell by the look on your face you were mesmerized by her, even though you had just met her. I'm so sorry, but as you said, perhaps it will be benign and it will all be over soon."

*　*　*

Paul stopped at the house. Without saying a word, he put his arms around Lucy. "Listen, Mom, you are the toughest woman I know and you have been through plenty of difficult situations before this. With God's help, you will come out on top this time, too. I have every confidence you will."

"Thank you, Paul. I am clinging to that hope. And to Cal," she added.

* * *

Tess declined the invitation to attend church with them on Sunday, saying she needed time to get her things together before flying home. Len stopped by the guesthouse when she was packing. "I wanted to bring these," he said as he handed her a bouquet of wildflowers. "I know you can't take them with you but they'll last for a few hours until you leave."

Tess took them and told him, "I've never received flowers from a man before. That was very thoughtful of you. Did my brother tell you they want me to move here? He and Lucy offered to find an apartment for me and help with expenses until I can find a job."

"What did you tell them?" Len asked her, trying not to smile too much.

"I promised I would think about it," Tess said. "I love living in New York. I'm not sure I could adjust to life in Texas. I don't know my way around, and I don't know the customs or the best shopping places and restaurants. I don't know any people here, except Cal and his family."

"You know me," Len said quietly, "and I'd be happy to show you all those places, if you'd let me."

"Oh Len, that is so sweet of you, but you really don't know me. We met just a week ago."

"That's true, but I've always been the kind of guy who can size someone up quickly. For instance, when I challenged Ms. Frasier to that shooting, roping and cutting contest, I knew she'd probably beat me. I could tell it in the way she carried herself and all that self-confidence she had. I know you're worried about something and I wish I could take that burden off your shoulders for you. I hope you decide to come back, Tess. Will you allow me to take you to the airport?"

Tess smiled at him. "Sure. That would be great and I would appreciate it."

She had said her goodbyes before Cal and Lucy left for church. There was nothing left to do but think. *Would she be happy here? Maybe. Could she force herself to take Cal's charity? Possibly, especially since she didn't seem to have much choice and they hadn't made it seem like charity, even though it was. Where did Len fit into her decision? He seemed like a nice guy but what did he want from her? She never had an honest-to-goodness boyfriend or a serious relationship of any kind. Her mother never approved of any boys who wanted to date her in high school, and later she managed to find something wrong with any man who seemed interested, too.*

Tess laughed out loud thinking what her mother would have to say about Len. It didn't matter now; she could like any man she chose and that was a freeing thought.

When they reached the security line at the airport, Tess turned to thank Len again for bringing her. Then for no apparent reason and before she could stop herself, she stood on her tiptoes and quickly kissed him before she disappeared into the line of passengers.

CHAPTER 23

"THE DOCTOR'S OFFICE CALLED this morning." Lucy told Cal when he came in for lunch.

"And?" he asked, waiting for her to continue.

"The surgeon and the radiologist have conferred. They want to do a needle biopsy instead of surgery. It's less invasive; it can be done as an outpatient with no anesthetic, other than on the site where they will insert the needle."

"That all sounds good, but the bottom line is whether or not it's as effective at determining cancer cells as the surgery. Right?"

"Yes, of course. Paul has been doing a lot of research online about our options. Perhaps we should talk to him and the doctor before consenting to the procedure," Lucy suggested.

She stood and walked to the window. "I'm so tired of thinking about it and all the 'what-ifs' involved. I feel like I'm losing my mind. I just want to know...now. Waiting is making me crazy."

Cal went to her. "I know, Honey. I want to know, too. Remember when you told me on several occasions that it's hard to fight an enemy if you don't know who or what they are? That's where we are right now. We don't know what we're dealing with. It will be resolved soon; at least we will know that part of it."

*   *   *

Jarrod and Doug came each day as promised and went to work, cleaning out the stalls. Although it was hard, there were no complaints from either of them. When Lucy took them some cookies and lemonade for a break, she noticed Jarrod wasn't wearing the gloves Cal had given him the first day. She turned his palms up and winced when she saw the blisters forming.

"Put the gloves on, Jarrod, and stop at the house when you're done today," she told him.

When Cal came home, he found the boys on the porch and Lucy massaging a healing ointment onto Jarrod's palms.

"I came to tell you boys what an excellent job you're doing," Cal said. "Judging from your hands, Jarrod, I would say you still aren't following instructions too well."

"No Grandpa, I guess not," Jarrod agreed. "It seems to go much faster if I don't wear the gloves."

Cal nodded. "I agree with you, but in the end, it will be slower because your hands will hurt so badly, you won't be able to hold that pitchfork or shovel. I'll call your Uncle Ben. While he's in town, he can pick up some smaller sized gloves. The ones I gave you are probably too big and that's why they feel clumsy to you."

After the boys left, Lucy said, "Rubbing that ointment on Jarrod's hands reminds me of a time when I saw *what love looked like* for my grandparents. Grandpa was the ultimate *man's man*. He loved the Lord and didn't drink or smoke but he was as tough as they come. He never asked any of his ranch hands to do anything he wouldn't do. He worked hard every day and his hands definitely showed it. My grandma always scolded him for not wearing his leather gloves when working, but he would say he couldn't work with gloves on.

Consequently, his hands were rough and cracked and looked like leather. Every night before they went to bed, Grandma would massage some healing lotion into the cracks on his hands. They would discuss the day while she gently rubbed his hands for a long time."

Cal said, "We all learn what *love looks like* from different situations, don't we?"

* * *

Tess met with Sandi after she returned to New York. She knew this would be a session of playing "Twenty Questions."

"Tell me about your trip, Tess. The last time we met, you weren't even sure you were going and then I get a message cancelling your next appointment because you're in Texas. What changed your mind?"

"I don't know, exactly. Maybe the notice from my landlord informing me I had one month left and would need to renew my lease or move. Or the stack of credit card bills in the mailbox or sheer desperation. Maybe all of the afore-mentioned things."

Sandi nodded. "I understand. Now tell me about your brother and the visit. Was it as scary as you envisioned?"

Tess shook her head. "No, it was good. Cal was a little hesitant when I first arrived but I think he didn't know how to approach a complete stranger, which is what I was, basically. His wife, Lucy, welcomed me with open arms and then Cal did, too. They were very good to me. I met the entire family; Cal's children and Lucy's and all the grandchildren. I wish I could go back in time and be in their lives when they were younger."

"You can't go back, obviously, but you have the option of going forward. Did you ask about moving there and if they would help you?"

Tess smiled. "I didn't have to ask; they volunteered to find me an apartment and a car and help me out until I could find a job. There were some strings attached, though."

Sandi raised her eyebrows. "Yeah? Like what? You wouldn't have to herd cattle, would you?"

They both laughed at the idea. "No, but I would need to agree to taking some money management classes and job skills assessment and training."

Sandi thought she liked this brother and his wife. Obviously, he got all the *life skills* in the family. "How do you feel about those requirements?"

"Truthfully, I would like to go on a shopping spree to make me feel better but that's impossible when I have no cash or cards."

"What else did you do while you were there?"

"I met Lucy's best friend, I learned to ride an ATV, I toured the ranch, I saw a family that sticks together, and I observed a love between my brother and his wife that I wish I could have some day," Tess said wistfully.

"Who says you can't? You're never too old to find the love of your life. Maybe there's a cowboy just waiting to sweep you off your feet, Tess," Sandi told her.

Tess tried not to smile but the corners of her mouth turned up involuntarily. "Maybe there is," she replied.

Sandi questioned her. "Does that look on your face indicate you've already found someone?"

Tess shrugged her shoulders. "Maybe. At least there is a man who seems to like me. I can tell you he's a bit rough around the edges and my mother would never have approved of him."

"You don't need your mother's approval any longer, Tess. You're an adult, a grown-up, a woman free to make her own choices. But...with that freedom comes the chance that you may have to live with the consequences of those choices."

"Yes, I know," Tess said quietly.

"One more thing, Sandi. I didn't have one headache while I was there. Do you suppose they are caused by stress?"

Sandi smiled at her. "It would seem so, Tess."

*　*　*

Vicki checked the caller ID before she answered the call. "Hello Uncle Leon. How are things in Colorado? Please tell me you have good news for me."

Leon hesitated. "Vicki, I wish I did. It seems we're dealing with an unreasonable judge on this matter. He has some unfounded fear that Blake is going to take off while I accompany him to Texas. I assured him I would take full responsibility for getting him there and back to Mountain House, but he's refusing to grant permission to fly on a commercial airline."

"Do you think he would allow it on a private plane?" Vicki asked. "I think I might be able to arrange that with the help of Cal and his friend. He could even land at the ranch where there's an old runway, if the judge doesn't want Blake anywhere near an airport."

"Let's check that out. You find out the information on your end and I'll see what can be done here with convincing the judge," Leon told her.

Vicki asked about his daughter-in-law's pregnancy and how she was feeling. She couldn't decide if she should tell Leon about her mother's situation or not, but made the choice to do so.

Leon was very quiet for a few seconds while he absorbed that information. "Thank you for telling me, Victoria. It will be another reason for me to come to Texas, soon. Good luck with the small plane idea. Please let me know as soon as you find out if it's a possibility."

*   *   *

Lucy lay on her back on a table while the radiologist numbed the site on her breast where he would insert the needle for the biopsy. They had used the information Paul found for them and asked for a biopsy that was used in conjunction with an ultrasound. That enabled the radiologist to make a more exact extraction of tissue from the lump in her breast.

Cal was allowed to stay with her. He held her hand and turned her face toward him. "Look at me, Lucy. He can do his work without you watching him. We'll spend this time making plans for our second annual November trip to Chicago with Jerry and Phoebe."

She turned her head to him and listened to his plans. When a few tears escaped and ran down onto the sheet, he wiped them from her face and continued to talk about where they would go and what they would do. It hurt his heart to see her sad and scared. She had never been frightened by anything in the years since he met her, with the exception of when he was shot. Lucy was nearly always in control of a situation, whether it was a striking rattlesnake, shooting an ex-husband bent on killing her, unscrupulous business people, threats or enraged bulls. She knew how to handle things and he loved that about her. This, however, was out of her control.

When the procedure was finished, they were told the results would be available in a week to ten days, another seemingly interminable wait.

*   *   *

"Cal?" Vicki said when he answered his phone. "I have a huge favor to ask." She recounted the conversation she had with Leon. "Would you consider asking your friend with the plane if we could hire him to bring Blake and Leon here and then return them to Colorado when the time comes for Devon's surgery?"

"Of course, I'll ask him. Simon is retired now and would probably enjoy flying somewhere for a purpose. I'll contact him and let you know as soon as I can."

* * *

A week later after meeting with the surgeon and discussing the results of the needle biopsy with him, Lucy lay in Cal's arms with her head on his chest. "You know, I was prepared to be devastated by the results, but then I was elated that the biopsy showed the lump was benign. Now the surgeon isn't totally willing to believe the results and he still wants to do surgery and remove the lump to be certain. I have never had my emotions go up and down so fast in such a short period of time, in my entire life."

Cal sighed. "I know. I was prepared to celebrate and now we'll have to wait again."

Lucy sat up and turned to him. "I was thinking, Cal, how we could end this whole merry-go-round and be certain of the prognosis no matter what the results are, good or bad."

He frowned. "How would that happen?"

"I've read about women who have a history of breast cancer in their family and they choose to have both breasts removed before there is a chance of them having it or dying from it. If you don't care what I look like, I think I'm going to ask the surgeon about that. What do you think?"

He pulled her back to him. "Here's what I think. Number one, you don't have a family history of breast cancer. Number two, no surgeon is going to agree to that operation without the test results which you would have to wait for, anyway.

Number three, you are tired and scared and impatient and grasping at straws. And last but not least, I wouldn't care a bit about how you looked because I didn't fall in love with you because of your breasts, ok?"

She chuckled, "Are you sure about that, Cowboy? I remember a night in my kitchen in Illinois when my silk pajama top slipped off my shoulder...."

Cal laughed at the memory. "I loved you for a lot more than that sight, Lucy, and you know it. It's good to hear you laugh, though." He kissed her and then said, "God says, 'This too, shall pass.' and it will. We will make it out of this valley of uncertainty, I promise."

CHAPTER 24

CAL TOLD JACKIE HE AND LUCY would be available to spend the weekend with the boys, if she and Gary would still like to have a mini-vacation.

The remodeling of a portion of their house was nearly completed. Gary's father would be moving in when it was totally done. Lucy was concerned that it would be too much of a strain on Jackie and Gary and the boys, but only expressed that opinion to Cal and not to them.

"How much care or supervision will Gary's father require?" Cal asked.

"I don't really know, but I think it's more than they perceive. The life of a caregiver is so taxing. I don't know how Jackie is going to give Gabe all the attention he needs plus this active little guy, too," she said as she picked up Michael, rescuing him before he fell off a chair he had climbed on.

Gabe was happy that he was coming to Grandpa Cal's house. Cal made sure he brought his guitar out where Gabe could see it. When Gabe became distraught about something, which could be often, he could sometimes be calmed if Cal played softly for him. The guitar seemed to have a mesmerizing effect on his over-stimulated senses. Michael didn't care where he was as long as someone fed him and played with him. The three days passed quickly and gave Cal and Lucy a chance to think about something other than the upcoming surgery.

"I'm exhausted," Lucy told Cal after the boys returned to their home. "Is that a sign I'm getting old? I used to be able to chase kids all day long. I couldn't do it anymore, that's for sure."

"You're not getting old; you're just out of practice. And kids are a lot different than what you're used to. You can still ride a horse or chase cattle all day, just not kids."

"If you say so, but I'm not convinced. Michael is a chunk. It's like lifting weights. I ache in places I didn't know I had."

Cal massaged her shoulders and back until she relaxed. "Mmmm, that felt so good," she told him. As she was drifting off to sleep, curled up in his arms, she mumbled, "Tomorrow, I'm going to take Danielle, our favorite female cowhand, shopping."

"What's she shopping for, exactly?" Cal asked, curiously.

"Something to make her look feminine so some young man, named Zach, will notice her, I believe. She's spent too long trying to make herself look like a boy."

Cal shook his head slightly. "I will never understand women, I guess." Lucy was asleep and didn't hear him. *'It's okay. I understand the woman in my arms and that's all that matters'* he thought.

* * *

Lucy took Danielle to several shops at the mall, but nothing seemed to suit her personality. Then Lucy remembered the small shop where Vicki used to work part-time. They had lunch on the way and discussed some things.

"I know you said you didn't think you would be hired if Cal or Ben knew you were a girl and I do understand that. In my former business, I felt the need to prove myself as qualified as the men, many times. But now, you don't feel that way any longer?" Lucy asked.

"Not nearly as much," Danielle confessed. "Your husband and Mr. Ben have given me the same responsibilities as any of the men. But, you know, some of the guys still don't think I can do the work and sometimes, they don't want me on their crew for the day."

"That will probably be slow to change, Sweetie. It may be unfair, but old stereotypes are hard to break. The best way to change their minds is to continue to do the work to the best of your ability. They'll eventually realize how qualified you are. That's true whether a woman is working in an office or on a horse. So, now I want to know about this Zach, who seems to have caught your attention."

Danielle blushed. "He was hired by the foreman a few months ago and he is one of the guys who doesn't mind if he works with me. Last week, he asked me to go to a movie with him but I realized I only own jeans and work shirts. I thought maybe I should wear something a little more feminine. I don't know much about fashion or girl clothes; I've been dressing like this since I was in high school. My mom died when I was little and my dad raised me. He's a great guy but he always dressed me in jeans, too. I never got to the *girl* side of the stores."

Lucy thought what a pretty young woman was hiding under the men's clothing. "Well, Danielle, let's find something that looks feminine but not *too* girly, okay? You don't want Zach to be so shocked, he doesn't recognize you."

Danielle tried on several things and settled on a pair of casual slacks and a soft blouse. She could still wear her dress boots and be comfortable.

When Lucy dropped her off, she told her, "Stop by the house before you leave for your date; Mr. Frasier and I want to meet this young man, okay?"

* * *

Cal sat in the waiting room during Lucy's surgery. He had finally run into a place he couldn't be with her. Even though he insisted, it was not permitted. When they finally told him she was in recovery, he couldn't get there fast enough. She was asking for him, although she had no idea what she was saying. He laughed at her ramblings and fed her ice chips.

The surgeon stopped by to say everything went well, although the lump was larger than he anticipated. She would have a 'dimple' or depression in her breast where the tissue had been removed, and a small scar, of course. His nurse would call with an appointment time when they could come in and discuss the results. He signed the release papers and Cal took her home.

*   *   *

Simon agreed to fly to Loveland and bring Leon and Blake to Houston when it was time for Devon's surgery. The judge finally agreed to those conditions. Leon was required to sign a waiver of responsibility for Blake's return to Mountain House.

"I'm not sure where the judge thinks Blake's going to go," Leon confided in Clint. "I suppose on the way to Houston he could make an attempt to get lost in the crowd, but on the way home, he's not going to be in any physical condition to bolt anywhere."

"How do you feel he's dealing with the whole scenario?" Clint asked.

"He seems to be frightened, of course. Who wouldn't be? But he also is happy he can finally do something good for one of his children."

"Do you know if Devon's parents have told him about his father being the donor or are they keeping that information a secret? I understand their dilemma. It would be a hard thing to explain to a six-year-old," Clint sympathized.

"I don't know what they've decided. I do know they've discussed it with a counselor and with their pastor. I'm sure Vicki and David have done a lot of praying about it, too. To add to the confusion, it isn't just Devon we're talking about. He's a bright kid and will know, of course, if that's *his* father, it is Bethany's father, too, and I'm sure he'll tell her. Bethany has enough adoption related emotional issues, I can't imagine what will happen if she suddenly meets her biological father."

"Life can certainly get tangled, can't it?" Clint observed.

Leon smiled and nodded. "You're looking at the *king of tangled*, remember?"

* * *

Lucy's phone rang. It was Danielle wanting to know if she and Zach could stop by the ranch house before going to the movie.

"Are we surrogate parents for these two?" Cal asked teasingly.

"Maybe," Lucy told him. "She doesn't have a mother and I want to see who Zach is. Do you know him?"

"No, I don't. I'll probably recognize him when I see him, but the guys don't wear name tags, y'know."

Lucy rolled her eyes at him and waited for Danielle and Zach to show up. She was happy to see Zach open the truck door for Danielle and have his hand on her back as they approached the porch where Lucy and Cal waited for them. It was nice to know he had some manners.

Zach shook hands with Cal while Lucy asked what movie they were going to see. She took Danielle aside while the two men talked and let her know she looked perfect for the evening.

After they left, Lucy asked Cal, "Do you recognize him now…even without a name tag?"

"Yes, I do. I'm not so sure about him though. He seems a little too 'slick' if you know what I mean."

"Do you think Danielle will be okay?" Lucy asked, concerned.

Cal chuckled. "I'm pretty sure he'll be looking at the stars if he tries anything. She's one tough little cookie."

* * *

When the day finally arrived to hear the results of the biopsy, Cal told Ben not to worry about them if they didn't return that night. He had plans to stay in town, whether it was to celebrate good news or cry over bad results.

They were ushered into the doctor's office. He placed his fingers together, teepee style and looked at Cal and Lucy over the top of his glasses. "First, I would like to apologize for the long wait you have endured. I am rarely wrong in my assessments of lumps. I could not convince myself to believe the results of the needle biopsy. That's the reason I insisted on the surgery, also. However, you will be relieved to know this time I was proven wrong. Everything came back benign. You have no cancerous cells, Mrs. Frasier."

Cal squeezed Lucy's hand so hard, her knuckles turned white. They left the office, and being conscious of others who had not received good news perhaps, they waited until they reached the street before he picked her up, swung her around and kissed her.

Cal drove to the hotel and parked. Lucy asked, "What are we doing here?"

"We are celebrating, Mrs. Frasier. Celebrating God's goodness, answered prayers, life in general and *your* life, specifically."

Cal called their children and Phoebe to let them know the results. He and Lucy held hands and strolled down the streets, basking in the sunshine. They sat on a park bench, contemplating how much better everything looked now. They thanked God for hearing their prayers. They found an Italian restaurant for dinner, and then went back to the room. "Since you planned this night, my love, did you happen to bring a nightshirt for me?" Lucy asked.

"I did pack one, but I don't think you'll need it," was Cal's reply.

Later, as she lay in his arms, sleeping peacefully, he cried tears of relief and thankfulness.

CHAPTER 25

LUCY MET PHOEBE FOR A CELEBRATORY LUNCH in Cypress at the Long Branch Café. They were in the middle of dessert when Lucy's eyes suddenly opened wide and she smiled from ear to ear.

"I've seen that look before," Phoebe laughed. "What's the great idea that just popped into your head?" she asked.

"I want to have a square dance at the ranch," Lucy stated as if she were talking about a sandwich instead of a big production.

"A square dance?" Phoebe repeated incredulously. "Who knows how to square dance?"

"It doesn't matter. The caller will teach people how to do the moves. It will be fun. We'll have it in the aisle of the stable or on the patio or on the old runway if we invite enough people for several squares. Ohhh, Phoebes, it will be such fun. I'll rent some of those big monster propane heaters, in case it's chilly. We'll make it our Christmas party and all the employees and their families will be invited and friends from church and Cal and Ben's business associates and…everybody. Won't it be fun?" she asked, as excited as a child about the plan.

"If you say so, Lucy. What exactly will we be celebrating?"

"Well, by that time, Devon's kidney transplant should be in the past and Tess might be living here by then. We can celebrate your clothing shop . . . and I don't know what else. Life, we'll celebrate life, our lives and the Life that came to earth at Christmas so long ago. How's that? Enough reasons?"

"Sure. It's your party. Have you talked to Cal about this wild idea?" Phoebe asked her.

"No, Silly. I just had the idea a few minutes ago." They both laughed. "I'm sure he'll be on board with it. Right now, our relief meter is so far off the charts, he would celebrate with fireworks if we had some."

Phoebe looked serious. "I know he would, Lucy. He talked to Jerry a few times when you didn't have the results yet. He was beside himself with worry. I know part of it was because of his first wife, but it was more than that. He told Jerry that you are the very air he breathes. I thought that was the most loving comment I ever heard."

Lucy glanced out the front windows of the restaurant to keep the unbidden tears from sliding down her cheeks. "Yes, that is pretty special, isn't it? I feel the same way. When I thought he might die after he was shot, I had no idea how I would go on breathing, either."

They were both lost in thought for a bit, when Phoebe remembered Lucy mentioning Tess moving to Texas. "Has she really decided to come and try it?" she asked.

"I won't know for sure until I get home. Cal was talking to her when I left. I think she probably will. Really, I don't think she has a choice. She has nowhere else to go, as far as we can tell. She didn't say that in so many words, but she hinted at it. No money, no resources, no vehicle and soon, she'll have no apartment, I believe. Keep your eyes open for a small house or apartment to rent here in Cypress or in Magnolia, okay?"

Phoebe nodded. "I wish I could afford to hire her to work in the clothing shop when I can't be there but since the women don't have to pay for the items, it's strictly a volunteer job."

Their conversation was interrupted when Lucy's phone rang. She glanced at the number and location, and then told

Phoebe. "I have to answer this. It's from Batavia, IL. Maybe it's my realtor."

"Hello? Yes, this is Louisa Frasier." She frowned at Phoebe and shrugged her shoulders, indicating she didn't know this person.

After listening for what seemed like an interminable time, she said quietly, "Yes, I do understand and I will call you back, Sergeant, after I see if I can make some arrangements."

Phoebe's eyes opened wide at the word, *Sergeant*. She anxiously waited for an explanation.

Lucy looked dismayed, surprised and disbelieving, all rolled into one. "That was a policeman from Batavia. I guess you were right about Anna being abused by someone. They found her, barely conscious and badly beaten, in an alley. She had no identification with her, but they found my card in the pocket of her jeans. Remember when you gave her my card because you didn't have any with you that had your name on them? He also found out I still own the store Anna rents. He would like me to come to Illinois." She thought for a minute, and then continued, "Maybe he thinks I had someone rough her up because of the rent she owes me."

"No, I don't believe that's what he thinks at all, Lucy. He probably wants to have your help finding information about her. And, since your card was with her, you're his only *lead*, as they say in the crime dramas on television."

Lucy grabbed her purse and the bill. "I have to go. Maybe Cal will go with me to Illinois. Better yet, pack your bags, Phoebe. You can come with me."

She called Cal to find out where he was and ask if he could meet her when he was finished with his paperwork.

* * *

"Hey, Babe, did you have a fun lunch with Phoebe? Are you girls planning our annual Christmas trip to Chicago in November?" he asked when he came in the door.

"I wish that's what we were planning," she told him. "Do you remember me talking about Anna, the young woman who makes and sells jewelry? She rents my building in Batavia and was considering buying it, although now she hasn't paid rent for a couple of months."

"Yes, vaguely. Wasn't she the one that Phoebe feared was being abused?"

"Same one. I received a call from a policeman in Batavia because she had one of my cards in her pocket when they found her beat up in some alley. She had no other ID with her, so they called me."

Cal frowned. "I hope they find whoever did it and hang him. What does he want you to do?" he asked her.

"I don't know that he wants me to do anything, but I feel I need to go there and rescue her somehow. Phoebe will go along if Jerry agrees. She's the one with all the contacts for abused women," Lucy explained.

Cal put his arms around her and looked in her face as she leaned her head back. "You know, Lucy, you are not required to rescue every person on the planet and some people don't want to be rescued. There are some things that can't be fixed."

She sighed and put her head on his chest. "I know, Honey, but if she has no one else, I can't just ignore the situation, and it would afford me the opportunity to put the building on the market while I'm there. I would really be happy to sever my last tie with Illinois, except for visiting there with you, of course."

"I'm concerned about your safety. How do you know the person won't come back to her shop and harm you? I think I need to go with you. Ben can handle everything here."

Lucy laughed as she said, "What? You don't think Thelma and Louise can take care of business?"

"Actually, I'm more worried about the trouble Thelma and *Louisa* can get themselves into," he confessed.

"I'm fine with you going along, Cal. Tell me how soon you can go and I'll get our tickets."

"We should probably go as soon as possible. When I talked to Tess, she said she'll be arriving by the end of the month. Obviously, that's when her lease is up or when she can't pay her rent any longer, I'm not sure which. I told her she will have to live in the guesthouse until we can find suitable housing in town. She seemed fine with that and I'm sure Len will be happy about it," he added, chuckling.

* * *

Ben and Cal had moved the Canoodling Hammock from the front porch, where it took up too much room, to the patio at the back of the house. As Lucy and Cal walked through the great room, she noticed Ben and Candy were making use of it, talking and snuggling. "All three children must be napping," she observed.

"Maybe they're considering number four," Cal said.

"Bite your tongue, Calvin Frasier," Lucy scolded him. "Maybe in the future, but Candy is still recovering every day from the twins' birth and her post-partum depression. I think getting pregnant would probably send her over the edge. Although they can practice all they want," she added.

Cal smiled at her words. "It's not like we have anything to say about it, anyway. That's their business, right? We can concentrate on our own practicing."

"That's true," Lucy laughed. "Although I'm not sure that we're *practicing* for anything. I think we have it down pat, Cowboy."

* * *

Cal, Lucy and Phoebe took a cab from the airport to the hospital where Anna was recovering. Although she was allowed to have visitors, Cal let Lucy and Phoebe go into the room to see her. The sight of her bruised and broken was more of a shock to Lucy than it seemed to be to Phoebe. Having lived the experience, she was prepared for it. She was also prepared for Anna's unwillingness to tell them what happened.

Phoebe stayed with her while Cal and Lucy went to the Batavia Police Department. They discussed the incident with the sergeant who called Lucy initially. He noticed the revolver Cal had with him, under his jacket. "I'm assuming you have a permit to carry that?" he asked. Cal nodded and provided the information.

The sergeant told them they had no idea what happened and Anna was not cooperating. Lucy explained that she owned the building where Anna had her business.

"I thought you looked familiar. You lived on Concord Avenue, right? I missed the connection because your last name wasn't Frasier then, was it?" the sergeant asked.

"No. It was Louisa Crowder when I lived here," Lucy told him. She provided the information she had when Anna originally rented the building, but she didn't know if that was still the correct home address.

When they left, Cal said, "It's too bad crimes can't be solved as quickly in real life as they are in movies and television programs."

Phoebe called and told them she was considering taking Anna home with her. She had already talked to Jerry about it. "She won't tell me who did this because she is too frightened and she can't go home. She has no one else here; what is she supposed to do?"

"I don't know, Phoebe. Do you think it's wise to move her so far away? She can't live at your house forever."

"I know, but she could stay until she can get some counseling and figure out what to do. She refuses to go to a shelter here because she says he'll find her. I'm afraid the next time he'll kill her, Lucy. I don't have a choice, do I?"

"Let me talk to Cal about this for a minute. I'll call you right back."

"Phoebe is considering taking Anna home with her. Jerry approves but she wants our opinion. We seem to be in the business of rescuing people lately and that's okay with me. God rescues us every day. What are your thoughts?" she asked.

Cal nodded. "As long as she asks the police before she whisks her out of here. They may want Anna here for more questioning. Also, what are you going to do about her shop? Can we pack up all her merchandise and supplies and somehow get it to Texas? We can't leave it here, and if you want to put the building on the market, it will need to be emptied."

Lucy called Phoebe and relayed Cal's advice. She also asked Phoebe if she thought Anna was up to the task of making rational decisions. If she was, Lucy wanted her to ask if she and Cal had her permission to begin packing her inventory and supplies.

Phoebe said she would talk to Anna about that and let her know. She also agreed to speak to the sergeant before she purchased a ticket for Anna.

They weren't returning home until the next day, so after Phoebe called and said Anna told her they could do whatever they wanted with her things, Cal and Lucy went to the store to see exactly how much would have to be boxed up and moved. Lucy used her key to unlock the door. She made certain the sign on the front door said 'Closed' when they went inside. That would eliminate any customers thinking it was open for business.

"I'm going to the basement to see if I can find some boxes to pack the jewelry. There may be some big enough to put Anna's supplies and equipment in, too," Cal said as he disappeared through the basement door.

"Thanks, Honey," Lucy called after him. "I'm glad it's you and not me going down there. I never did like that basement."

Cal returned with an armload of smaller boxes. "These should get you started," he said as he handed them to her. "I'm going back to see what else I can find."

Anna had an old-style combination radio and tape player on the counter. As Lucy turned it on for some background music, she thought that she had not seen one of those for a long time. Young people didn't even know what a cassette tape was. This one seemed to work perfectly and the tape had country western music on it. She hummed along as she proceeded to open the glass showcases. She wrapped some of the pieces in tissue before placing them carefully in a box.

She heard the tinkle of the bell on the door and without turning around, she said, "I'm sorry, but the shop is closed."

Chapter 26

"LOUISA?"

The hair on the back of Lucy's neck stood up as she recognized that voice. She turned and stared into the face of the man who once worked closely with her in her development business, until she terminated him.

"Hello James," she said casually, as though she wasn't surprised to see him in Anna's shop. She had learned a long time ago never to allow her surprise, indignation, or any other emotion show on her face if she wanted to maintain the upper hand in a situation. "What are you doing here?"

"I came because Anna called me a few nights ago. I told her I couldn't come to her rescue again but I was in the area today and thought I would stop to see if she was okay."

Lucy's senses were on high alert. She didn't trust him any further than she could throw him. "How do you know Anna?" she asked, as she continued to sort and pack jewelry.

James walked over until he was standing next to her. "Well, to tell you the truth, I was pretty upset with you when you fired me. I knew you owned some property in Batavia and I knew you wanted to sell it. I thought if I posed as a dummy corporation, I could buy it for a fraction of what it was worth and then I would feel as though I put one over on the mighty Ms. Crowder."

Lucy looked him in the eyes and said, "You really thought it would affect my financial bottom line if you bought this property for a lowball price?" She shook her head and laughed at the idea.

He shrugged his shoulders. "No, I'm sure it wouldn't. But it would have given me some satisfaction. Things didn't work out that way, though. I met Anna and I liked her. I gave up on my plan of revenge. We dated and I thought we had something special."

"What happened?" Lucy asked, still trying to decide if he was telling the truth or fabricating an elaborate lie.

James shrugged his shoulders again. "She suddenly didn't want to see me anymore. She had some new guy. I think he was abusive to her. She called me several times and said she was scared. I would go to her apartment and check it out for her, but this time I didn't go." James looked around. "Is she here? I came to apologize for not rescuing her again."

Not trusting what he was saying, Lucy answered, "No. Anna isn't here right now. I'm helping her by packing up some of her things. I was willing to sell this building to Anna for a price lower than you could have hoped for, James. Anna has decided she isn't interested so I really do want to sell this property now and it needs to be emptied."

"Do you know what she needed when she called? Was her boyfriend hurting her again?" James asked as he looked around the small storefront.

He sounded sincere, but she had misread his intentions when he worked for her and she wasn't going to let that happen again.

"I have no idea what she wanted when she called you, James. I wasn't even aware that she *had* called you. And I don't know where she is"

His eyes narrowed as he looked at her. "Come on, Louisa, who do you think you're talking to? You've never been involved in anything unless you know all the details. You know where she is or you wouldn't be here packing her stuff."

"I told you I'm helping her pack because she doesn't want to buy this building. If you're not dating her any longer, why do you want to know where she is so badly?" Lucy asked him. "Furthermore, why do you care?"

He hesitated, as though he was trying to come up with a believable answer. "I loaned her some money and I came to pick it up," he said as he turned and walked toward Anna's cash register. "Did she leave any cash in here?" he asked as if talking to himself.

Lucy stepped in front of him, blocking his path. "You are not going to take anything from this shop unless Anna says you should have it."

"Well, she's going to have a hard time giving her permission from a hospital bed isn't she?" he said smugly.

Lucy smiled slowly and reminded him, "I thought you didn't know where she was, James."

His lip curled a bit as he looked at her. "I don't know for sure; I just assumed if she got herself beat up again, she would probably be in the hospital."

"What happened to you, James? When you worked for me, you were always a bit pushy, but you were good at your job and I trusted you. I don't recognize the James who tried stealing my financial information before I fired you or would even dream of beating on a woman. Who are you?"

"I'm the man who wanted you desperately when I worked for you, but you always kept me at arm's length, like I wasn't good enough for you. I'm the man who had huge gambling debts and you ruined the only way I had of paying off my creditors when you fired me. I'm the man who still has debts and really doesn't care about any of the people who get in my way, including that stupid little Anna. She could have helped me by buying this building when you offered her a low price, but she refused," he answered. "I pretended to like her and care about her and she still wouldn't help me out. She was talking about morals all the time and how it wouldn't be right to cheat you since you had been so kind to her. The whole thing became tiresome and disgusting."

"Well, aren't you just the charmer of all time, James? So, when Anna wouldn't help you, you decided to beat her up? Did you think she was going to be able to help when she was unconscious?"

He smiled a sleazy smile. "You'd be surprised how fast a few bruises can make someone change their mind, Louisa. And don't even think about shooting me like you shot Derek." His eyes checked her over as he asked, "Where you keepin' that little pistol you carry, Louisa? I know you have to be able to get your hands on it to pull the trigger. I'm not as stupid as Derek."

Lucy laughed. "That fact might be debatable. The good thing is you're standing a lot closer to me than Derek was. I could drop you like a rock, James, and I wouldn't even have to aim and for beating up Anna, I really should."

He grabbed both of her wrists and held her arms in front of her. "You're not going to shoot anybody as long as I keep your hands out of your boots, purse, pockets, or anywhere else you might be hiding that Smith and Wesson."

Lucy kept her eyes on James' face, although she was aware Cal had come into the room from the basement. "I suggest you take your hands off my wife," Cal said in a measured tone that left no doubt about his intentions.

James turned his head to see Cal standing behind him. Even though Cal had his hand on his pistol, James continued to hold Lucy's wrists. While his head was turned, she brought her knee up with as much force as she could. He released her arms and crumpled to the floor.

Cal shook his head and smiled at her. "You're so dramatic, Honey. I'm pretty sure I had his attention. I wasn't going to allow him to hurt you."

"I know....that was for Anna," Lucy told him. "I'm going to call the sergeant and tell him we have the person who was harming her." She looked down at James as she stepped over him. "You disgust me, James."

He gave her a lop-sided grin. "Anna will never testify against me or identify me as her attacker. I promise you that."

"We'll see, won't we?" Lucy said as she used her phone to call the police station. She proceeded to walk to the counter where Anna's old radio was located. She popped open the cassette door and took out the tape. Looking at James, she said, "You're slipping, James. You didn't even notice when I pushed the *record* button and the music stopped playing. You just confessed and it's all on tape. Anna won't have to identify you."

* * *

Cal and Lucy stayed an extra day to pack Anna's things. They made arrangements for everything to be shipped to a storage unit near Phoebe's shop. Phoebe stayed with Anna until she was released from the hospital and could take her back to Texas. The police were aware of her contact information and they had the tape, so consequently, they allowed her to leave the state.

Lucy placed a call to the realtor she had used in the past. "Dana, this is Louisa Frasier. It used to be Louisa Crowder. Yes, it has been a while, hasn't it? Do you remember my building on Main Street? I want you to put it on the market. Almost any offer will be accepted. I believe you still have a key. The truck will be coming to pick up the boxes we have packed and they will pack the remaining items, so you will need to unlock the door for them, if possible. It will have to be cleaned, I'm sure. I'd like to leave it in your hands; you have my phone number if you need anything. I'll be back in

November. If it has sold by then, I can sign any papers you have. Thank you."

She took Cal's arm as she surveyed the inside of the store. "This is the last tie to my life in Illinois. I will be happy when it's sold."

"Are you sure you won't be a little sad to have no ties to the places you know so well?" Cal asked her.

Lucy pulled him close and kissed him with every ounce of passion she had in her. "I know you so well, too, Calvin Frasier, and I belong in Texas with you. Understand?"

He nodded his head. After he recovered his voice, he told her, "I understand perfectly, Lucy, but in case I forget, will you remind me like that when we get back home?"

* * *

Cal and Lucy's flight from Illinois arrived at the airport ahead of schedule. Ben was coming to pick them up but when Cal called him to tell him they were there, Ben said they would have to wait for a bit anyway. "Candy just called and said Tess is arriving on a flight from New York in an hour so you and Lucy may as well find a place to wait. I'm not leaving without all three of you," Ben laughed."

"What?" Cal asked. "She wasn't going to get here for another week."

"Let me guess," Lucy said after he ended the call. "Tess is arriving today."

"Not just today, but in an hour," Cal affirmed. "Let's grab our luggage and find something to eat while we wait for her to arrive. I'm starving." He took her arm and guided her through the crowds to a restaurant. "I'll text Ben and tell him where we are," Cal said.

"Did you let Tess know exactly where we are, too?" Lucy asked. Cal nodded before taking another bite of his sandwich.

"Yes. They should be able to find us after she claims her bags. I'm anxious to get home and I'm sure Tess is, too. Did we really leave Texas just a few days ago? It seems like weeks."

Lucy watched as Cal devoured his meal. She believed this man could eat half a beef if someone fixed it for him. While smiling about that thought, Ben walked into the restaurant carrying one bag while Tess pulled a rolling suitcase.

"Tess. I'm happy to see you made it in one piece," Cal told her as he pulled out a chair for her. "Are you hungry? Order anything you want. I know they don't give you much but peanuts or crackers on flights anymore."

"I don't need anything to eat, but I am really thirsty," she said. "Ben might be hungry. He's been lugging that bag around and it's heavy, I know."

Cal glanced at his son and started to laugh. "Ben? Hungry? Surely not."

"Come on Ben," Lucy told him. "Order what you want. Tell your dad if he wants a ride home, the driver needs to be well-fed."

Tess laughed with them and said, "I love the way your family teases and jokes. I didn't realize what I was missing until I saw it in action. I've never experienced that kind of family interaction."

Becoming serious, Cal told her, "This *is* your family now, Tess, so get ready for all sort of interactions."

*   *   *

After everyone finally made it back to the ranch, and Tess was settled in the guesthouse, Lucy snuggled against Cal on the couch. Before they could talk, her phone rang. She checked the number and recognized it as Leon's.

"Hi Lucy. I have good news and maybe some 'not so good' news."

Lucy laughed. "That's what every person wants to hear when they answer the phone, Leon."

"I know," he agreed. "I'm sorry. The good news is Devon's surgery is scheduled for next week. Cal's friend, Simon, will be picking Blake and me up on Monday. The other news is this: Do you think it would be possible for us to stay at the ranch for a few days before the surgery? Simon said he can land the plane on the old runway at the ranch. Blake of course, has no insurance and David and Vicki haven't received an answer yet from their carrier about all the extra expenses. If we can avoid a week's worth of hotel bills, that would be very helpful. Vicki and David have plenty of room, but in light of the circumstances, it wouldn't be a good idea to stay there."

Lucy had switched her phone to speaker mode so Cal could hear the conversation. He was nodding his head at her, indicating she should say yes. "Yes, Leon, that will work. The guest house is taken but the two bedrooms upstairs are available. Is Blake sure he wants to stay at our house? As I recall, he still remembers when I threatened to shoot him."

Leon was laughing and in the background, Blake was, too. "He says he will sleep with one eye open, Lucy."

* * *

"Do you think things will ever settle down for us?" Lucy asked.

"I don't know," he replied. "We seem to float from one event or catastrophe to another. Float probably isn't the correct word. Sometimes, it seems we're pushed. But I think Hotel Frasier is full to capacity now, so I don't believe there can be any more guests arriving."

"Perhaps we should put a 'No Vacancy' sign on the gate at the end of the drive. I feel as though we haven't had time to breathe, or stop long enough to catch our breath," Lucy sighed. "By the way, I heard that you told Jerry I was the very air you breathe. That is possibly the most romantic and touching thing I have ever heard."

Chapter 27

"CAL, HONEY...I had an idea the other day," Lucy said as she smiled at him across the table.

"I know I'm in trouble when you use that tone," he laughed. "What was this great idea; even though I'm afraid to find out?"

"How do you feel about a square dance?" she asked.

"Sure. Tell me when and where. I like to square dance, although I haven't done it for a while. It will be fun."

Lucy laughed the throaty laugh he loved to hear. "What? Why are you grinning like that? Did I miss something?" he asked.

"Yes, Cal. It was a loaded question to begin with. I'm sorry. I want to *have* a square dance here at the ranch and make it our Christmas party. We'll invite our family and the employees and their families and your business associates and their families and our friends and..."

"Take a breath, Lucy or you'll pass out from lack of oxygen." He stood behind her and massaged her shoulders. "I think it's a great idea. Were you worried that I wouldn't want to do it?" Cal asked her.

"Maybe...a little," she admitted. "But I was going to try my best to persuade you to see it my way."

"Lucy Mae," he scolded, using the name he alone was allowed to use. "When have you ever had to persuade me to do something? I can never say no to you and you know it."

"You're right, Cal. You've spoiled me rotten and I love every minute of it." She pulled his arms down until he was close enough to kiss on the cheek. "Now get out of here. I've kept you from your work long enough."

*   *   *

Lucy called Phoebe. "Can you meet me for lunch? We have some serious planning to do. By the way, how's Anna doing?"

Phoebe told her to stop at the clothing shop. She would order pizza and they could eat while they worked and talked.

When Lucy walked in the door, she was happy to see Anna sorting clothing. "Well, you look much better than the last time I saw you, young lady," she told her.

Anna smiled but didn't say anything. She continued working as Phoebe gave Lucy a task to do while they waited for the pizza to be delivered.

"Phoebe, we have so much to plan for; I think we need tons of lists. Cal says I am the Queen of Lists," she laughed.

"What is this "we" stuff? What am I planning for, Lucy?" Phoebe teased.

Lucy's eyes opened wide. "You are going to help me plan for this Christmas square dance, aren't you? Oh please say yes, Phoebe. Between that and our trip to Chicago in November and Devon's surgery and Hotel Frasier being filled to capacity, I need your expertise and advice."

"I was only teasing you, my friend. I would love to help. Planning things is one of my best skills. Did you ask Cal about the square dance?"

Lucy nodded. "Yes, just this morning and of course, he said it was a good idea. Well, let me rephrase that. He didn't exactly say it was a good idea; he just said I should go ahead and do it."

Anna brought a picture over to where they were talking. "Someone obviously thought an abused, homeless woman needed a large picture for her non-existent wall," she said sarcastically as she held it so they could see it. "It was in that large box of donations."

"Hmmm, it's a lovely picture," Phoebe observed as she looked at it "We'll keep it in the back room for now. If one of the women rents an apartment, perhaps she would be able to use it."

"Maybe you should have it appraised, Phoebe," Lucy said as she perused the other things in the box. "Look at the clothing that was in that box. Those are high-end goods. Perhaps the picture is worth something. It is an oil painting."

"Why would someone stick a valuable painting in a box of donated clothes?" Anna asked.

Lucy shrugged. "Who knows why people do things? Maybe they were cleaning out a house and didn't know the value of it, or perhaps they just wanted to be rid of it. I'll volunteer to take it to a photographer I know, who also deals in paintings. Is that okay with you, Phoebe?"

"Sure. Take it anywhere you want. Now, let's discuss this square dance. The first thing you need to do is choose a date, then find a band and caller…is that what you said the guy is called?" she laughingly asked Lucy.

The pizza was delivered and they ate it while making plans. "Anna, have you heard anything from the police in Batavia? Will you have to return?" Lucy asked.

Anna shook her head as if trying to erase all the memories. "I don't have to return, at least not now. The tape you gave them was enough to press charges. I never thanked you and your husband for helping me with all the packing and paying to have my things moved here."

"Thanks aren't necessary, Anna. We want you to heal and you wouldn't even have met James if it wasn't for the fact he knew me and was looking for revenge. Some people change when they're desperate."

Anna looked at Lucy and told her, "I will make up the rent I owed you, too. James forced me to give him the money I would have sent to you. I'm truly sorry."

Lucy moved to Anna and put her arms around her. "Please don't give it another thought, Anna. I will survive without your rent money and hopefully, the building will sell soon and that will be the end of that story."

When Anna left to run an errand for Phoebe, Lucy asked how she was adjusting.

"She seems to be adjusting to the situation really well. I'm sure she would rather not be living with Jerry and me, but for now, that's the only option. Truthfully, it has been an adjustment for us, too. We were pretty used to having the entire house to ourselves. Now we have to stop and think about things like dashing from the shower to the bedroom without a robe. Y'know?"

Lucy laughed at that picture in her mind. "Yes, I do know. We have enough people and grandchildren with us most of the time that I can relate. Speaking of that, Leon and Blake are coming to stay until the day of the surgery. That should be interesting, considering one of the last times Blake and I saw each other, I was threatening to shoot him."

Phoebe spit soda everywhere, laughing at that statement. "And he's still going to stay at your house?" she asked.

"Desperate times call for desperate measures, Phoebe," Lucy told her. "He doesn't have a choice and he is going to save Devon's life. That's a pretty big deal."

They finished compiling the list of calls Lucy needed to make for the square dance and discussed the November birthday trip to Chicago. Lucy wrapped the painting and left, saying she would let Phoebe know what her photographer friend said about it.

* * *

She thought she might as well stop at the photography shop while she was in town, hoping Craig would be there.

"Hello, Lucy. How can I help you today?" Craig said as she entered the shop.

"I would like your opinion of this painting. Not an actual full-blown appraisal, just a quick observation," she told him as she handed it to him.

While Craig looked it over, she wandered around his store, looking at examples of his amazing and unorthodox photography. An idea was brewing in her mind and it made her smile, just thinking about it.

"I can't really tell the worth," Craig told her, "but I am positive it's not a run-of-the-mill painting. It definitely has some value but I would need to have a colleague do some research and a full appraisal to know for sure. It seems as though I've seen it before, somewhere," he said thoughtfully. "Perhaps it will come to me."

"You can keep it here and I'll pay for the appraisal. If it's worth something, Phoebe's shop could use the money. Now, I want to discuss something else with you. While I was admiring your unbelievable skill as a photographer, I had an idea for a Christmas gift for Cal and all of our children's families. You can tell me if it's a possibility or not."

They discussed what Lucy envisioned. Much to her delight, Craig told her it was not only possible, but he would love to do it. She gave him the names and numbers of each family and told her she would let them know he was going to call them.

* * *

When Lucy returned home, she had to scoot several pairs of boots off to the side to get in the door. It made her smile to see Luke's little boots next to Ben's big ones, and the sight immediately brought back many memories. Other than bare feet, boots had definitely been her only footwear when she was a child, and now she seemed to have come full circle in her life and in her choice of what to wear on her feet.

Thinking about the boots, she had another idea form in her mind. She called Craig to let him know the photos were getting more complicated. He laughed and said, "I'm always up for a challenge."

Tess joined Lucy and Cal for dinner. "I am beyond grateful to both of you for allowing me to stay here and putting all my things into storage, but now what happens? I can't just twiddle my thumbs all day, every day," Tess lamented.

"You're right, Tess," Cal told her. "But you might have to be patient for a little while until we can make some arrangements for you to have your own apartment and a vehicle and a job of some sort. It won't happen overnight, although that would be nice, wouldn't it?" With a serious face, he said, "Or maybe I could find something for you to do that required you to ride one of the ATVs again."

Tess stuck her tongue out at him. "You are never going to let me forget that day, are you, dear brother? I think I should learn to ride a horse. That would probably be more comfortable than one of those ATVs."

"I bet I can think of someone who would love to teach you to ride, Tess," Lucy grinned.

Tess's face turned red. "If you mean Len, he has already offered. You two are such matchmakers, aren't you?"

Cal and Lucy both laughed at her. "No, we don't mean to push you and Len together, Tess. You seem comfortable with each other and that's good. You both could use a good friend who is not related to you," Lucy explained.

After dinner, as they cleaned up the kitchen, Lucy's phone rang. "Lucy, this is Craig. I remembered where I saw that painting. When an elderly, wealthy widow died several months ago, there was an estate sale. I attended and bought a few pieces. That painting you brought in was there, also. Obviously, no one purchased it and her relatives must have boxed it up with the other things that didn't sell and were donated."

"Are any of her relatives living in the area?" Lucy asked.

"I don't think so. If I'm not mistaken, they all live out east somewhere. The house is up for sale too, but the realtor is having a difficult time selling it. It is way too big for most families as a single dwelling, and at some point, it was remodeled to have apartments on the upper floor with the main floor kept as her living quarters. The story is that she needed the apartments for someone to live there and keep an eye on her as she got older but she wanted to stay in her own home so she kept the main floor as her own. I'll let you know if I remember anything else."

Lucy smiled at Cal and put her arms around his neck. "How would you like to part with some of our money and become landlords at the same time? I think I may have just learned something that could solve a lot of problems."

He kissed her upturned face and almost forgot what he was going to say. He regained his composure and asked, "You don't think we have enough problems with all the things that go on here at the ranch? Now you want to add some more by becoming landlords of property in town?"

Lucy returned the kiss and said, "That's my story, Cowboy, and I'm stickin' to it."

Chapter 28

AFTER CAL LEFT the next morning, Lucy asked Tess to help her get the upstairs bedrooms and bath ready for Leon and Blake. She filled Tess in on the circumstances surrounding Devon's kidney transplant and the nearly impossible odds of finding a donor. She stressed that it was only by the grace of God that Blake was found and was a match.

"Does Devon know Blake is his father?" Tess asked as she pulled the sheets off a bed.

"No, he doesn't," Lucy explained. Devon knows he is adopted and he's pretty mature for his age. I think he could handle that information. However, he would also want to tell his sister, Bethany, and she might not be able to process it. She has had some emotional problems since she first joined Victoria and David's family and is just now beginning to feel loved and accepted. I don't know what suddenly meeting her biological father would do to her."

"Have you and Len gone on any more dates?" Lucy asked, admitting she was being nosey.

"Not exactly a date, I guess. But he has come over to watch some TV with me on several occasions in the evening. It seems silly for two people to sit alone in their own houses when they could enjoy each others' company, doesn't it?" she asked Lucy.

Lucy smiled at her and nodded. "Certainly seems like a good idea to me."

* * *

"David, what are we going to do if Devon wants to know who Blake is?" Vicki asked as she put Olivia's pajamas on her, despite the little girl's squirming and loud objections.

"I don't know, Vic. We've been wrestling with this ever since we found out who the donor was. I've prayed for wisdom but I don't feel any closer to being wise about this situation than I did when I began."

Vicki put Olivia in her bed and kissed Devon and Bethany while David said prayers with them.

Vicki got into bed with David. "Hold me tight, Honey," she said as she pressed her body against him. He wrapped his arms around her and held her as she spoke her fears out loud. "I am so afraid. I worry about the operation itself and about Devon's recovery and about Blake and if he will say something about being the kids' father and of course, about his recovery, too and..." David put his finger to her lips. "Shhhh, Sweetheart. Stop talking. You and I have the same fears but we can't control what will happen, no matter how we try. We will still be a family, regardless of what is or isn't said to Devon. God has us all wrapped up in his arms just as I have you in mine right now. We have to trust him to be in charge, okay?

"Mmmm-hmmm" Vicki agreed as David kissed her.

* * *

Lucy contacted all of their adult children. She asked each family to set an appointment with Craig, the photographer, when he called. He would tell them what he wanted them to wear and where the photo would be taken. She also asked them not to tell Cal about it. Now she had to figure out some way to get Cal to the photographer to have their picture taken without making him suspicious. There was plenty of time to think of something, and she was grateful to think that Devon would be recuperated before their picture session.

* * *

So she wouldn't be frightened, Cal had warned Tess about a small plane landing on the old runway, which was not too far from the guest house. Jarrod and Annie came over to see Simon, the pilot, and Luke was so excited by the whole thing, Candy had to hang onto him or he would have been headed for the plane while it was still moving. There was no fear in that little boy and it scared Lucy sometimes.

Cal had come in from working to be there when Leon and Blake arrived. He invited Simon to stay for dinner and he gladly accepted the invitation. Lucy was happy about that, thinking the more people who were there, the less awkward it might be for Blake.

When Ben entered the room, the two men stared at each other for a minute, each one remembering the last time they met. Ben's stern look became a smile as he held out his hand and told Blake how happy he was about what he was doing for Devon. Blake seemed to relax as the conversation continued, and they all enjoyed dinner.

After dinner, Lucy found Blake on the front porch. She sat down across from him as she sized up the man he had become. "I know how uncomfortable it must be for you to be here, Blake. Once I held a gun on you, and the next time, I was threatening you when I came to see you in jail. Leon has told me how you've turned your life around and I'm happy for you. How do you feel about it?"

Blake took a deep breath and then answered her, slowly. "I want to apologize for the trouble I caused when we met the first time. I believe that portion of my life is in the past. I thank your brother and God for the changes in me. I'm also thankful I can help Devon." He looked past Lucy and out across the yard. "I wish with all my heart I could have been a father to my children, but it wasn't meant to be. You were right when you told me it only took fifteen minutes to make them and then I disappeared. I'm very thankful they have your daughter and son-in-law to be their parents," he said quietly.

Lucy had to fight the urge to hug him as she would one of her children who was hurting. After all, she could be his mother; he wasn't as old as her children. Instead, she assured him she and Cal would keep him in their prayers, not just for the time of the surgery, but for all time. She questioned him about his plans for the future when he would be leaving Mountain House. Blake shook his head and cleared his throat. "I don't have anything permanent planned yet," he said. "Leon and Pastor Clint are working on some job opportunities for me. Most businesses won't hire someone with a felony on their record, but Mountain House seems to find the places that are willing to take a chance on us."

Everyone retired early as they had to be at the hospital in the wee hours of the morning. Lynne was going to watch Bethany and Olivia. David had asked Cal and Lucy please to come to the hospital and sit with him and Vicki. Leon would be there, too, of course.

* * *

Devon was such a trooper. Most kids would have been scared to death, but he seemed to think this was a great adventure and was in a happy mood. Perhaps he knew he would feel so much better after the operation was over and could return to a normal life. The doctors had done a terrific job of explaining the entire procedure to him, using drawings and words a child could understand. The recuperation time was much faster for the recipient than it was for the donor.

When it was time to be wheeled into surgery, Blake and Devon were on gurneys next to each other. Devon turned his head to look at Blake. "Hi, Mr. Tanner. My name is Devon."

Blake smiled back at him. "Nice to meet you, Devon. Are you ready to get this over with?"

Devon nodded his head. "Yes. Thank you for giving me one of your kidneys. I know they're important and not many people want to give one away. What made you decide to give one of yours to me? Do you know my mom and dad?"

Vicki grabbed David's hand and waited for Blake's answer. Blake looked at them and then back to Devon. "I'm a friend of your mother's Uncle Leon. He asked me to help." A tear slipped down the side of Blake's face as they wheeled them both into the operating room.

*   *   *

It seemed like an eternity before the surgeon appeared to speak to them. He told them everything went like clockwork and he was very pleased with the results. Both patients would be in the recovery room in a few minutes and then moved to their separate rooms in ICU when they were stable.

Cal and Lucy left when Devon was in his room. There wasn't room for everyone, and Vicki and David were the only people he needed to see. Before they left the hospital, they stopped by Blake's room too, just to let him know they were thinking about him and praying for his recovery.

*   *   *

Their first stop on the way home was at the house Craig had told Lucy about. They met the real estate agent for a tour. It was a huge house and at one time had probably been magnificent in its grandeur. The floors and woodwork were all hardwood. The front entrance and stairs looked like something from the movie, *Gone with the Wind*. Cal went to the basement to see if it was dry and check the water heater, furnace, and anything else he could find. The main floor consisted of a living room, parlor, dining room, a huge kitchen with a pantry, a bath, and a room that had been converted into a bedroom for the previous owner. Upstairs there were three apartments, all of which were fairly large.

They discussed the asking price and what might be accepted by the sellers. Cal suggested they discuss it for a few days and pray about it before making a decision. The realtor assured them it probably wasn't going to be sold in the meantime, since they were the only interested party at the moment.

As they drove home, Cal said, "I can tell by the look on your face you like it a lot, right?"

She reached over to him and rubbed his cheek. "You know I do, Cal. But we both know I tend to follow my heart these days instead of my head, like I used to do."

"Yeah, Baby, what happened to that wickedly powerful businesswoman who stole my heart?" he asked.

"She fell in love with some handsome, sexy, loving cowboy and hasn't been the same since," she answered.

* * *

Cal stopped at the end of their drive to get the mail. He handed it all to Lucy except a letter from the local cattle association. After he read it, he handed it to her. "They're putting a directory together and want a picture of all the members and their spouses. We don't have a recent picture of us, Lucy. Do you think your photographer friend, Craig, could take one?"

Lucy just looked at him with her mouth open. *Wow, God. I didn't expect an answer to my prayer about a picture of us to arrive so quickly.* "Yes, I'm sure that could be arranged," she said, grinning like a Cheshire cat.

* * *

Devon was released to go home after a few days in ICU. Blake was required to stay longer and then needed to stay at the ranch for another couple of days before they released him to fly home. He would be monitored at the hospital in Colorado for the remainder of his recovery time. Leon was anxious to get back to work and to Ginny.

* * *

Phoebe and Anna came for lunch so Lucy could discuss the house in town with them. She invited Tess, too. "I want to tell you my idea and get your opinions," Lucy said. "None of this is written in concrete and it is subject to revision. In fact, we haven't even made an offer on the property yet." She continued, "Cal and I looked at a huge house in town. There are three apartments upstairs and the main floor is beautiful. Cal and I would like to purchase it. Phoebe, that would allow the women who come to you and have nowhere to go when the shelter is full, to have a place to regroup. Tess, if you would consider occupying the entire first floor, you could be the 'housemother' for lack of a better term. I am fully aware of all the problems that could arise and the rules and regulations and the zoning issues. That is, or was, my area of expertise, so I'm not worried about handling that. What I want from you, is the assurance you will think about it, before we make an offer."

Anna was the first to speak. "I think it would be wonderful. I appreciate Phoebe and Jerry's hospitality more than they know, but they can't take every abused woman into their home. I think an apartment-type setting would be ideal."

Phoebe's brow furrowed. "What about the women whose abuser is still looking for them? How would we keep them safe?"

"Unfortunately, this wouldn't be appropriate for them. They would need to be at the shelter where they would be safe. I envision this as a place for a woman to live while she looks for a job, gets some education if needed, and then looks for other housing. We would not be in the business of keeping them safe."

Tess agreed to think about it. "So, you're saying I would have a place to live and would be earning some money by taking care of the place. Is that right?"

Lucy nodded. "Yes. I don't have that all figured out in my head yet, but I would want you to be in charge of the entire house. Make sure smoke detectors are working, have repairs done, and be there when someone moves in or out. I'm not being naïve. I know some of the women will take anything they can get their hands on when they leave, but I would want you to do a thorough background check, Tess. You are good on the computer and you have good people instincts, I think. It would be a selective process."

Anna wandered outside to get some fresh air. She sat down by Blake who was also enjoying some sunshine. They talked about their lives like they were old friends, perhaps because they knew they would probably never see each other again. It was easy to be open and honest with a stranger.

CHAPTER 29

SIMON FLEW IN TO TAKE Leon and Blake back to Colorado. Lucy hugged Leon when she said goodbye and then hugged Blake, too. "We will never be able to repay you for saving Devon's life, Blake," she told him with tears in her eyes.

"Perhaps someday when he's older and can understand, I will be able to tell him and Bethany I'm their father and I loved them, even if I didn't know how in the beginning," he said quietly. "I do have an address now, so maybe Victoria and David could send me pictures again, once in a while."

"I'll tell them, Blake. I'm sure they will do that," Lucy assured him.

* * *

The house seemed strangely empty and quiet after they left in Simon's plane. Cal and Lucy remained on the patio. Cal lay down in his hammock and pulled Lucy in with him, under protest. "Cal, what are you doing? We have to have our picture taken this afternoon. There's no time to take a nap in your 'canoodling' hammock."

"Who said anything about taking a nap?" he asked. "I just want to relax for a few minutes and I want you with me. There's plenty of time to get ready for Craig. Besides, you don't need to get ready; you're beautiful just as you are."

Lucy lay with her head on Cal's chest, listening to his heart beat. "I love you, Calvin Frasier, more than you will ever know," she said softly.

He tightened his arm around her. "I know, Lucy. I do know."

* * *

They relaxed for a while, and then changed into the clothes they would wear for the pictures. Cal brought Cutter and Harmony out of the stable when Craig arrived as he suggested the horses should be in the photo, also. He had Cal and Lucy stand and sit in various poses, all informal and casual.

While Cal took the horses back to the stable, Lucy took Craig to the house. She had two pairs of work boots on the porch, hers and Cal's. "Can you get a shot of these boots before Cal comes back?" she asked.

He worked quickly, placing the boots in different positions. "This is going to work out perfectly, Lucy. Maybe you should come to work for me as a consultant. I like your ideas and creativity."

"Thank you for the compliment but no, thank you, to the job offer. I have more to do than I can accomplish now," she said.

As Craig drove away, Lucy saw Ben drive up to his house on the other end of the patio that separated the two homes. "What are you doing here?" she asked, as he usually wasn't home until time for dinner.

Ben answered as he hurried inside, "Candy called and said there was an emergency but it wasn't the kids, so I don't know what it is, but I rushed home to find out."

Lucy continued to her house to change out of her *picture clothes,* knowing Ben or Candy would come over to explain the emergency when it was convenient. The house didn't seem to be on fire and if it wasn't about the babies, every other emergency could be handled.

When Cal returned, Ben met him on the porch. "Frank had a near-fatal heart attack. He has had the surgery and is in intensive care in Houston. Candy's brother, Steve, called to tell her. Candy says she doesn't care, but I know she does."

Cal tipped his hat back and scratched his head. "What's he doing in the hospital in Houston? I thought Frank and Myrna moved to New Mexico after they remarried."

"I asked Steve the same thing when I called him back. I guess they made the decision to relocate to the Houston area, just in case they were ever welcome in Candy's life again. They would be closer to her and the grandchildren," Ben said. "They are both retired, so they can live anywhere they choose."

"So, what now? You can't force Candy to go see him but I think she should. If he dies, she will regret not going and making an attempt at some sort of amends," Cal told him.

"I don't know, Dad. They nearly killed Candy with their confession right before she had the twins. I don't think I've forgiven them, if you want to know the truth," Ben said quietly.

Cal put his hand on his son's shoulder. "I understand, Ben, I really do, but holding on to your anger only hurts you, not Frank and Myrna."

Ben nodded. "I know that, but thinking about almost losing Candy and the twins is a powerful motive for staying angry." He glanced toward the house. "Candy is on the phone with the counselor she's been seeing about the family issues. If she makes the decision to go to the hospital, can we leave the children with you and Lucy?"

Cal nodded his agreement. "Of course."

When Ben called a few minutes later to tell Lucy of their decision to go to Houston, she suggested they leave the children where they were and she and Cal would come to their house. It would simplify taking care of them to have all the things they needed available without moving them.

A few hours later, Cal lay on the floor letting Sophia and Samuel try their best to climb on him, and Luke followed Lucy around the kitchen while she prepared dinner. "Luke, Grammy is going to step on you if you don't move a bit. What's wrong, my sweet Luke? Are you missing Daddy? I know you are his shadow, everywhere he goes. He'll be back soon. Why don't you ask Grandpa to read a book to you?"

Luke stomped out of the kitchen. With his chubby legs, it looked more like a shuffle than an angry stomp, but it made Lucy laugh as she returned to her cooking.

"Cal, can you bring Sophia and put her in her high chair? Bring Luke, too and I'll get Samuel," Lucy called a few minutes later.

"Sure, but Luke's already in the kitchen with you, isn't he?" Cal asked as he scooped Sophia up with one arm and used his other hand to grab Samuel.

The sudden terrified look on Lucy's face answered his question. "Luke?" she called as she went from room to room. Then she noticed the patio door was open just a crack, an opening big enough for a little boy to squeeze through if he was intent on going out.

"Oh, Cal, do you know how many places he could be? I should have checked to make sure the door was locked. I'm going to find him," she said as she reached for her boots.

Cal grabbed her arm. "Take a deep breath, Lucy. He can't have gone very far. You stay here with the twins and I will find Luke. I promise I won't come back without him, okay?"

"Okay," she whispered, as she felt her heart pounding in her chest.

She spooned pureed sweet potatoes into the twins' mouths as she prayed. *'Please, Lord, direct Cal's footsteps to Luke. Please keep him from harm and danger. Bring him back, Jesus, please.'* There were so many places he could be and most of them were not necessarily safe for a two-year-old.

Lucy had finished feeding Samuel and Sophia and was preparing bottles of breast milk Candy had in the freezer when she heard the front door open. Cal entered with Luke on his arm, sporting a dirty face with some lines where the tears had left clean rivulets down both cheeks.

"Where did you find him?" Lucy asked, while saying prayers of thanks that he was safe.

Cal looked at Luke. "Tell Grammy where you were, Luke. Where did Grandpa find you?"

Luke's bottom lip quivered, as he said, "Daddy's horse."

Lucy's eyes opened wide. "He was clear down by the stable where Ben keeps his horses?" she asked.

Cal nodded. "Yep. I found him sitting in the aisle outside the stall door. Evidently, he thought if he stayed by Ben's horse, he'd be there when Ben came home."

After she put Luke in his pajamas, she placed him on Cal's lap. He snuggled as close as he could and said, "I love you, Grampa." Cal kissed the top of Luke's head before reading a story to him.

* * *

Ben kept his hand on Candy's back as they entered the hospital. When they reached the Coronary Care Unit waiting room, he held her hand. When Myrna saw Candy, she excused herself to get a cup of coffee. Steve came toward Candy with his arms out. She allowed him to hug her, but she didn't say a word to him. Ben asked, "How is Frank doing?"

Steve shook his head. "Not so good. They had to do a triple by-pass operation. He was making progress but then he developed blood clots in his lungs and some inflammation in the sac around his heart. It will be a while before he is back to normal. Candy, you can go in to see him if you want to. He doesn't open his eyes, but the doctor said he can most likely hear us."

Ben felt Candy's whole body become tense. She took a deep breath and entered the room where Frank lay. A person would have thought he was dead if the lights on the ventilator had not been blinking.

Candy sat next to the bed and looked at Frank. She finally took his hand and stroked it. Ben couldn't hear what she was saying to him, but soon, he saw her shoulders shaking uncontrollably. He opened the door and led her out of the room. She clung to him and couldn't stop crying. Ben wasn't sure if her tears were because Frank might die or due to her distress about the lies that were told. He took her out to the hallway.

"Candy, Honey, we can go home. I can't bear to see you like this. You don't have to put yourself through this kind of stress again. I'm afraid you'll be sick. We can pray about your father's recovery from home. You don't actually have to be here."

She loosened her grip on his shirt and wiped her tears with her hand. "No, Ben, I have to do this. I'm strong enough to do this. I can't leave here without talking to Myrna, too. I want to talk to her alone, but please stay close so I can draw strength from you."

Ben walked with her to the cafeteria where Myrna was sitting at a table by herself. He sat at a table a few yards away while Candy walked to her and sat down.

"Myrna, I have to talk to you. I can't continue to carry this burden of hurt around with me any longer."

"Okay, Candy. But you don't have to put yourself through this. I understand and I promise I will stay out of your life."

"Please just let me talk before I lose my courage. We've already established the fact that I am not your daughter and I don't foresee us ever being best friends, but you are married...again...to my father and although he hurt me terribly with his lies, he was a good father to me when I was a child. I asked God why he allowed you to treat me the way you did. I know you were in pain, too. If Ben came to me with another woman's baby, I don't know what I would do. I've been to counseling and cried until there are no more tears to cry. I am offering my forgiveness if you are willing to take it. I'm praying Daddy recovers and will be able to see his grandchildren and watch them grow up. I don't want you to stay away when he comes to visit. You are welcome at our home." She turned to look at Ben, who was nodding at her, hearing her words.

Myrna had huge tears rolling down her cheeks. "I don't know what to say, Candy. I don't deserve your kindness, much less your forgiveness. You are a much better person than I am."

"God forgives me for all my sins, Myrna. Because of that, I have to forgive others. It has taken me all these months to realize that, but I knew it when I saw Daddy lying there, so still. I hope he heard me when I told him that."

She stood and walked to Ben. "Let's go home, please."

Chapter 30

"GUESS WHAT JUST HAPPENED," Lucy told Cal as he came in the door.

He laughed. "I'm always a bit hesitant when you meet me at the door with those words, Lucy." He took his boots off and sat down. "Okay. I'm ready. What happened?"

"The realtor called. She sold the property in Batavia. Isn't that great? And since they want to make use of it immediately, I can sign all the papers electronically. In a few days, I will be free of any ties to my former life in Illinois. Get up, Cowboy, and dance with me."

Cal laughed and twirled her around the living room. "I don't suppose the nice chunk of money you got for it is adding to this euphoria?" he teased her.

"Well, maybe a little. I think it will more than cover the cost of the house we looked at," she confessed.

"I knew there was a reason for your enthusiasm, more than just selling the property," Cal said as they both collapsed onto the couch, with Lucy ending up on his lap and his arms around her.

"Whew. I'm out of shape if just dancing around my living room makes me breathe this hard," Lucy said.

"I was hoping it was your partner who was making you breathe that hard," Cal replied.

"Yeah, that, too," she told him. "Anyway, how do you feel about the house in town?"

"It's your money, Lucy…"

"Stop right there, Cal. We agreed a long time ago there was no 'your money and my money' remember? This money is yours too and I want your advice."

"Well, it would provide a job for Tess and a good investment. The inspection came back looking good, so I vote 'yes,' okay?"

Before they could stand up, Tess knocked on the back door. "Come in," Cal called.

Tess looked at them tangled up on the couch and said, "Was this a bad time?"

"No, not at all," Lucy assured her. "We were discussing some news I received today."

Tess burst out laughing. "It must have been good news to celebrate that way."

They all laughed. "Just think what we would be doing if it was *really* good news," Cal told her.

"Oh, stop it," Lucy scolded as she stood up. "What can we do for you, Tess?"

"Well, I came to tell you I probably won't be moving into the main level of that house if you buy it," she said nervously.

"Really, Tess?" Lucy frowned. "Why not?" Did something happen to change your mind?"

"Sort of," she hesitated. Then she blurted, "Len asked me to marry him and move into his house; well, really, it's your house, but you know, it's sort of his house, as long as he works for you, I guess."

Cal and Lucy stared at her. "Forget about whose house it is. I'm still stuck back at the part where he asked you to marry him," Cal said.

"Tess, are you sure about this? I mean, you haven't known each other very long and you'll be stuck out here with no shopping or all the other amenities of living in town. Do you know him well enough? I thought you two were having a date every now and then and suddenly, you're going to marry him?" Lucy asked, incredulous at the news.

Tess sat down. "I know all the arguments against it, but we've talked a lot. He knows all my weaknesses and I know about his. We decided it was ridiculous to keep spending our evenings alone when we could spend them together and enjoy all the other perks of being married, if you know what I mean." Her face turned all shades of red.

Cal was trying desperately to keep a straight face, but finally started laughing. "Oh Tess, yes, we know what you mean and neither of you are teenagers, so you are free to choose the person you love without anyone interfering. If you and Len are sure about this, Lucy and I give you our blessing, although you don't really need it."

"One more question, Tess. You're not marrying Len because you know Mom would be very disapproving of him and you want to thumb your nose at her, posthumously?"

"I considered that, Cal, but the answer is no. I'm marrying him because I love him and he loves me and I've never felt this wanted or loved in my entire life."

"That's all the reason you need," Lucy told her. "When are you planning to do this?"

"As soon as you and Cal can stand up for us. We'll go to the courthouse for the ceremony. We'll keep it simple."

Cal looked at Tess. "Don't ever tell Lucy the words 'keep it simple' because she will make it a celebration, whether you want one or not."

After she left, Lucy's phone rang. She listened, and said, "That is wonderful. I'm so excited. Does he think he can sell it for that price? Thank you, Craig."

She followed Cal to the kitchen. "More good news. The painting that was donated...the appraiser says it is worth more than $10,000. Phoebe's shop just got a big boost in income."

*   *   *

Later that evening, she called Leon to see how Blake was healing. When she hung up, she told Cal, "Blake is doing well. The doctors have released him to Mountain House to finish his recovery time. Leon asked if I could get Anna's address for Blake. He would like to write to her."

"So, we've gone from being Hotel Frasier to Frasier's Matchmaking Service?" Cal asked.

Lucy shrugged. "I have no idea. For once, I had nothing to do with any of these situations."

*   *   *

As Craig took the pictures Lucy wanted, she went to his shop often to choose her favorites of each family. She almost always ended up in tears by the time she was finished.

"My work doesn't usually affect people this way," Craig said.

"I know. I am so pleased with your photos and the way you placed the children in each one and the images of the boots are exactly as I envisioned them. They are superb, Craig. Cal is going to love them and just looking at them makes me realize how blessed I am. These are happy tears."

"It was your vision, Lucy. I'm impressed with the boots addition. These should look great on the wall."

*   *   *

Lucy persuaded Len and Tess at least to have a reception at the ranch. After all, Len had been an employee for many years. His friends and co-workers should get to celebrate with him. She arranged for a light lunch and a big cake. Tess looked beautiful in a simple blue dress and Len wore a matching blue shirt. They refused Cal's offer to send them on a honeymoon, saying they would be happy going home to their house.

*　*　*

When the deal was finalized for the apartment house, Lucy asked Lynne to help her with choices in furniture and other things it needed. They spent a month making it look like a home.

"I want it to be homey, but not fussy. Most of the women who might come here to live for a while have nothing, so I want to be sure there are plenty of towels and supplies but not a lot of unnecessary things. They just get in the way," Lucy said.

"Since Tess got married, who is going to be in charge and live on the main floor?" Lynne asked.

"God has such a way of taking care of things, Lynne. Anna was going to use one of the apartments but now she's going to be the one in charge. She can continue with her counseling and earn some money, too. Plus, she will have time to resume making her jewelry. Tess is going to help Phoebe at the shop. Now that the money from the painting provided a little breathing room, as far as finances go, Phoebe can pay Tess to help her and be in charge while we run off to Chicago."

"And how is Candy's father?" Lynne wanted to know.

"Frank is recovering, slowly. He's home but is very limited in what he's allowed to do and he can't go anywhere so Candy and Ben took the children in to see him last week. That's a situation I never thought would be resolved but once again, God sees things differently than we do."

"Is God helping you with your plans for this square dance, too?" Lynne teased her.

"I certainly hope so, or I'm in big trouble," Lucy laughed. "I think I'm closing in on the arrangements. I will send invitations early so people can put it on their calendars. I have the huge gas heaters rented if they're needed, I have the music and the caller lined up, but I'm still working on the food. I want Dolores and her husband to enjoy themselves, not have to work, so I have to find a caterer to make all of it and deliver it."

"Changing the subject, we went to visit at Vicki and David's house last week. Devon looks wonderful. His appetite has returned and his energy level is way up. If you didn't realize he had an operation, you really wouldn't know it," Lynne said.

"I know. It is a miracle, isn't it?" Lucy agreed. "Another reason to celebrate when we have the party."

* * *

"Phoebe, are you ready for our Chicago adventure?" Lucy called as she stepped into the clothing shop.

"Yes, ma'am, I am," Phoebe told her. "Tess has everything she needs to keep things running smoothly here at the shop, Anna is all set at the house, and Jerry and I are looking forward to some much needed alone time."

CHAPTER 31

THE TWO COUPLES MADE RESERVATIONS at the same hotel where they stayed the previous year. They walked the decorated streets and window shopped, but bought very little. Lucy wanted to stop at the jewelry store again, to tell Vincent how much her daughters appreciated the necklaces he made for them last year.

When he saw them walk in, he greeted Cal and Jerry like long lost friends. "Hello, Mister Frasier and Mister Walker. It is a pleasure to see you both again."

Lucy looked at Vincent. "You don't have a hello for me after all the business we did in the past?" she teased.

"Yes, yes, of course, Miss Louisa. I always have time for you, and your friend, but today, it is the gentlemen who are doing business with me. Come with me, please," he said to Cal and Jerry, leading the way to a back room. "Mr. Watkins, the piece you want is for Christmas, correct? And Mr. Frasier, you are picking yours up today?"

"I guess we get the chopped liver treatment, Phoebe. I can't imagine what they are purchasing, but if it's from Vincent, it will be exquisite, I guarantee it," Lucy said.

They left the jewelry store with nothing more being said and no hints about the purchases.

* * *

Michigan Avenue was beautiful as always. This year they visited Magic Hedge, a bird sanctuary by Montrose Harbor. Walking along the lake and watching the waves crashing against the sea wall was a magnificent sight, but extremely cold if any of the spray hit you. They made it back to the hotel in time for dinner.

"This year, I have the use of both hands, so I can get dressed by myself," Lucy said from the bedroom.

When she entered the suite, Cal took a deep breath. "You get more beautiful every year, Lucy. I want to sit here and feast my eyes on you for a few minutes."

"Why, Mr. Frasier, you certainly have a way with words. You make a girl feel positively giddy inside," she said in her most exaggerated drawl.

He stood and took her into his arms and kissed her as passionately as he could. When he let her go, she said, "Okay, now *that* makes me feel giddy inside, Cowboy."

He smiled and took her hand. "Come on, let's have dinner. Then I have a surprise for you."

They met Phoebe and Jerry downstairs for dinner and a glass of wine. They danced to the sounds of an orchestra playing big band songs, interspersed with Christmas tunes.

Cal checked his watch. "It's time to go, Ladies. We'll get your coats and gloves."

Phoebe looked at Lucy. "This is exciting, I love surprises especially romantic ones," she giggled.

As they stepped outside, the doorman said, "Your chariot awaits, folks. Enjoy your evening."

A white Cinderella carriage being pulled by two white horses stopped in front of the hotel. The driver helped the ladies step in while Cal and Jerry climbed in next to them.

There were heavy lap robes to keep them warm and a box of chocolate-covered strawberries for each couple to enjoy while they rode slowly through the decorated streets of downtown Chicago.

Jerry opened a bottle of champagne and Cal poured it into long-stemmed glasses. "Happy birthday to the love of my life," Cal toasted. "I cannot imagine my life without you, Lucy, and I don't want to."

After the carriage ride was over, the two couples parted and each went to their own room. Cal asked Lucy to come sit by him. He handed her a small wrapped package. "Happy birthday, Lucy."

She unwrapped it with shaking fingers. Then she opened the velvet jewelry box. Inside were earrings with yellow diamonds set in a rose pattern. She sucked in her breath. "They are absolutely gorgeous, Cal."

"Before you say anything, Lucy, I want you to know I remembered every word you told me last year when I wanted to name one of our ranches the Yellow Rose again. I understand why you didn't want to do that. But I don't want you to dismiss the good memories of the Yellow Rose completely from your mind. I thought these would match your engagement ring and keep the name alive, in your heart."

"You are the most romantic man I have ever known, Cal. I thank God every day for you and it isn't because you buy me diamonds. It's because you are the air that I breathe, too."

The trip was over all too soon and they were on their way back to the warmer climates of Texas. "I had the best time, ever, Cal," Lucy told him as she put her head on his shoulder. "I don't know how you're going to top this trip, but I have faith that you will try."

* * *

The Christmas season was approaching quickly. Nearly all the people Cal and Lucy invited had accepted the invitation. Leon and Ginny even decided to celebrate in Texas. They arrived a few days before the party and surprised everyone by bringing Blake with them. Obviously he and Anna's letters were becoming more frequent and he wanted to see her again.

Leon explained there was a slush fund at Mountain House that could be used for variables at his discretion and since Blake's probationary time was over and he was now employed for several hours each day, the strict rules about his leaving the premises had been relaxed. Leon thought Blake deserved a reward for opening the door so hard he stopped Bruce from harming anyone. Clint and Janet couldn't come because the baby was due soon and her doctor wouldn't allow her to travel.

Lucy asked Leon if he would like to ride with her to see the headstone that had been made for their parents. Leon couldn't do it when he was there months ago with Blake. His orders from the judge had been explicit. He could not leave Blake's side.

Leon and Lucy stood inside the area surrounded by the wrought iron fence. Leon knelt and ran his fingers over the carved letters.

"Are you okay with this, Lucy?" he asked. "When we talked in Colorado, you were still clinging to your Yellow Rose memories."

"I've made peace with my memories, Leon, just as you suggested. I'm content to be a Frasier and live on the Frasier Ranch. I don't want anything else."

He hugged her. "I'm happy to hear that. And I'm happy to see the headstone. As you said, now there is a record that our parents lived and died. I'm not trying to be morbid, but will you and Cal be buried in this little plot, also?"

Lucy smiled. "Yes, we will and at the same time. You see, we've been asking God for a long time, if it's his will, that we enter heaven together because we can't bear to think of not being together."

"You do have a special kind of love, Lucy. I am very happy for you and for Cal."

They rode back to the house in silence. Leon had not been on a horse for many years and was enjoying the time.

*   *   *

The day of the square dance arrived, sunny and crisp. Lucy was sure that by evening their guests would be appreciative of the gas heaters. Before anyone other than their family arrived, Lucy asked them all to come to the great room. The entire brick wall was covered with a long cloth, meant to hide what was behind it. Craig was standing on one end.

Lucy said, "Okay, I have something to say, as usual," she joked. "Cal, this is your Christmas gift from me. And there is a smaller one for each family." She helped Craig take the cover off the pictures. There was a photo of each of their children and their families. Every one was different and unique. They were all dressed casually in jeans, shirts and boots and seated or standing either on bales of straw or in the yard at their house or in a park. On the end of each photo was another image. This one was of each family's boots, lined up, laying sideways, scuffed and dirty, working boots. Even the babies: Olivia, Michael, Luke and the twins had their little boots in the photos. On the wall, there was also the picture of Cal and Lucy with Cutter and Harmony accompanied by a photo of their boots.

"Craig, I hope you brought about a thousand business cards with you," Paul said. "When the guests see these, you will be a very busy photographer."

Cal was speechless. He continued to look at each picture for long periods of time. He stood close and then backed up to look at each one from a different angle. He took Lucy's hand as they walked up and down in front of the wall.

"What gave you the 'boot' idea?" Cal inquired.

"The afternoon I had to scoot Ben and Luke's boots aside to get in the door. I realized the one thing that signified my 'riding through life with you' was our boots. Every one of our family members had a pair and they could all say they were riding through life with the people they loved, even if it wasn't on a horse."

"How did you get these all hung without me knowing about it?" was Cal's next question.

"Craig helped, and Len and Leon, too; they were all in on it. My job was to keep you out of the great room."

"Hey, you two, get out here. You get to dance the first set and show us how to do it," someone called to them.

"Come on, Baby, we're going to a square dance," Cal said as he pulled her outside and stood on one side of the 'square' that was formed. They remembered all the moves and could swing, promenade and do-si-do. After several dances, Cal and Lucy left the square and allowed some others to dance. Lucy observed Blake and Anna walking together, holding hands. Danielle and Zach were dancing in the same square as Alisha and Toby and Jerry and Phoebe. Len and Tess had even been persuaded to try it, as well as Leon and Ginny. Jarrod and Doug found enough nerve to ask two young girls to dance, and Annie and Amy were drinking punch with a group of boys and girls. Lucy had hired some teens from church to watch the little children so Ben and Candy, Vicki and David, and Jackie and Gary could enjoy the evening, also. Lynne and Paul, Samantha and Sean, and two more couples from church formed a third square.

"I think your idea is a hit with everyone, Lucy," Cal told her as they sat out for a while.

"It looks like it, doesn't it?" she answered.

Before the evening was over and when the caller was taking a break, Cal took the microphone and asked for everyone's attention.

"Lucy and I want to thank y'all for coming tonight. We appreciate your friendship and hope you have a good time. I would also like to take a minute to thank our Lord, whose birthday we are celebrating soon, for his unending blessings to us, and there have been a lot of blessings in the past year, including successful surgeries, twin grandbabies, and my sister, Tess, came back into my life. But, as soon as we got to know each other, my foreman stole her away and married her. We have made some new friends and celebrate our old friends. The Frasier Ranch has the best employees in Texas and we appreciate you and the work you do. Before I forget, I want you to know you will find your Christmas bonuses in your next paycheck. Now, we ask God's blessings on each and every one of you and your loved ones in the year ahead. Merry Christmas."

The festivities wound down and people started to drift to their vehicles to go home. Leon and Ginny went to the guest house. Blake was staying in the upstairs room where he had stayed when he came before the operation.

After everyone left, Lucy asked Cal to come to the stable with her. "Another surprise?" he asked.

"No. I want to spend the night at the cabin with you. Let's saddle Cutter and Harmony and ride."

"Are you sure?" Cal asked her. It's awfully late...it's after midnight." When she nodded her head, he said, "Okay, Lucy. I would never turn down a chance to ride with you - day or night."

As they rode slowly through the fields, lit only by the moonlight, Lucy said, "I consider my life with you as one long ride, Cal. I may stray off the beaten path occasionally, but as long as you are riding by my side, I can always find my way back. I know I tell you often how much I love you, but I want you to know, you are my whole life. To borrow your phrase, you are the very air I breathe. Several years ago, when Phoebe dropped me off at the airport, she told me I should *bring a cowboy home*. I found my cowboy but he brought *me* home instead. I have been *loving that cowboy* and *riding with that cowboy* ever since. I intend to continue that ride through this life and into eternity."

When they reached the cabin, Cal helped her slide off Harmony. He put the horses in the lean-to.

"It might be chilly in the cabin, Lucy Mae," he told her as he opened the door.

"I'm counting on you to keep me warm, Cowboy," she said as she lifted her face to him for his kiss.

KEEP READING FOR A SNEAK PEEK OF
SAVING A COWBOY,
BOOK FOUR IN THE MAGNOLIA SERIES

CHAPTER 1

"LYNNE," PAUL CALLED FROM HIS OFFICE, with a note of desperation in his voice. "Do you know what happened to the files I had ready last night? They were right here on the desk and now they are nowhere in sight. They represent a month's work and I have to leave soon."

Lynne came through the door and perched on the edge of his desk. "Calm down, Sweetheart. I'm sure they're here. You probably just misplaced them. You know the kids wouldn't touch them and I haven't been in your office. So, unless there is a gremlin in the house, I'm thinking you are the last person to have them."

Paul took a deep breath. "Yes, you're probably right. I will replay my movements since I went to bed last night and see if that jogs my memory."

Lynne stood and moved to where Paul was standing with his eyes closed and his hands on his hips, obviously concentrating. She encircled him in her arms and kissed him. "Does that help your memory?"

He laughed at her. "It definitely brings back some memories of last night, but none of them have to do with red file folders."

Paul nuzzled her neck and whispered, "I wish I didn't have to go today. I have grown very fond of working from home and even though I have to travel to Houston only once a month, I would rather skip that, too, if I could."

Lynne looked up at him. "I know but it is only one day. You will be back this evening, right? Or are you staying over and coming home tomorrow?"

He sighed again and shrugged his shoulders. "I really don't know. If all the presentations go according to plan, I will be home today, but if they get behind, then I may have to stay. I will call and let you know."

As Lynne moved away from him, she glanced down into his briefcase. "Hmmm, red file folder. Imagine that." She pulled it out and handed it to him.

"I think I'm losing my mind, Lynne," he said as he shook his head. "Obviously, I put it in there last night before we went to bed. It's inconceivable to me that I wouldn't remember that. I think I need to ask Mom if dementia runs in our family."

It was Lynne's turn to laugh at him. "Don't be silly, Paul. Your mother is 63 and I don't think there is a shred of any forgetfulness in that brain of hers. She seems to be on top of things all the time. And when she speaks of her grandparents, your great-grandparents, they were fully functioning until the day they died."

"Okay, I guess you're right. I'm just nervous about this day and the importance of the work I've been doing." He closed his briefcase and carried it with him to the kitchen.

"I have time for a cup of coffee with you before I go," he said as he sat down at the table.

Lynne poured two cups of coffee and sat across from him. Paul Newsome was a handsome man and she loved him with all her heart. She was thrilled five years ago when they moved into the house on the second ranch that belonged to Paul's mother, Lucy, and his stepdad, Cal Frasier. Even though her parents were in Illinois, Lynne had never felt more at home than she did here in Magnolia, Texas. The children felt that way, too. They had lived their first years in Batavia, Illinois, just a few houses away from Lucy. When she married Cal and moved to Texas, they were devastated. Paul's work moved them to Oklahoma but when he had the option to work from home, Cal and Lucy suggested they move into the ranch house and this had been home ever since.

"We haven't talked about your photography classes, Honey. I've been so engrossed in this job for the last month, I'm afraid I've neglected you and Jarrod and Annie. After today, I will have free time again. Perhaps we could take a short vacation. How does that sound?"

"It sounds wonderful, Paul, but I don't think you are going to pry Jarrod and Annie away from their 'jobs.'"

He smiled. "They do have a work ethic, don't they? Jarrod is so happy to be on the payroll at the ranch. Ben says he does an excellent job and works hard all day. I think the cowboy gene skipped a generation, going directly from Mom to Jarrod. I never thought horses and cattle and sweat and dust were appealing, but Jarrod does, and he is only thirteen years old. I am amazed."

Lynne took a swallow of her coffee. "And Annie is just as diligent about helping Candy with the children. Luke is four and a half and the twins are three. With the addition of Garrett a few months ago, Candy and Ben need Annie's help. She's a ten-year-old nanny, sort of."

Annie bounced into the kitchen. "Good morning, Daddy. Why are you all dressed up in a suit so early?"

Paul hugged his curly-haired little princess. "I have to go to Houston today and meet with a bunch of people about the project I've been working on. I was telling your mother maybe we could take a short vacation next week. What do you think?"

Annie shook her head. "Oh no. I can't leave now. With the new baby, and the twins and Luke, Aunt Candy really needs me. I don't know what she'd do without me."

Paul smiled at Lynne over the top of Annie's head. "I guess your mother was right when she said you and Jarrod couldn't leave your jobs. I think I will take Mommy on a trip for a few days, just the two of us. How does that sound, Annie?"

"Sure, go ahead. I can sleep at Grammy's house and be close to the kids as soon as I wake up. And Jarrod won't care as long as he can follow Uncle Ben around on his horse."

Paul stood and checked his watch. "I have to go or I'll be in more traffic than I want to be. Is Jarrod still here so I can say goodbye or has he already left? I know these *cowboys* start work at the break of day."

Annie answered his question. "He left a couple hours ago, Daddy. I'll tell him you said goodbye if he and Uncle Ben come in for lunch, okay?"

"Okay, Sweetie. I'll drop you off at Ben and Candy's on my way. But first, I need to tell your mother goodbye."

"Listen, Lynne, I was serious when I said we would take a few days and go somewhere nice. You can take that new camera and practice all the photo techniques you've been learning in Craig's classes, okay?"

She placed her arms around his neck and kissed him with the kind of kiss that would make him remember all day who he was coming home to.

"Mmmmm, if you keep that up, I will never get to Houston," he said in her ear.

"Okay, go and be careful. I will pray God keeps you safe on the roads and in the meeting and that all goes well."

"Thanks, Lynne. God is always in charge. I will call when I get there and again when I'm on the way home. I love you."

She watched him and Annie leave. They drove down the drive and out of her sight.

She thought to herself. *'Be with him as he makes his presentation, Lord. Take good care of him and bring him back safely.'*